"Hey," the cab driver yelled, "come on, my friend, quick!"

The two motorbikes were closing on them. They'd hit the brakes as the cab came to a halt, but were skidding on the loose surface of the road, fighting to keep control.

Bolan flung open the rear door, catching bike and rider full-on.

"My cab!" the driver cried in anguish, but it didn't stop him from doing likewise, his own door catching the second biker and spinning him into the low brick wall of a yard where goats bleated in fright at the impact.

The cab driver muttered a prayer as he hit the ignition. "Now I will take you to your meeting, Captain America."

"Why are you helping me?"

"You will hear from me again. Do not worry about that...."

MACK BOLAN ®
The Executioner

#347 Dragon's Den
#348 Carnage Code
#349 Firestorm
#350 Volatile Agent
#351 Hell Night
#352 Killing Trade
#353 Black Death Reprise
#354 Ambush Force
#355 Outback Assault
#356 Defense Breach
#357 Extreme Justice
#358 Blood Toll
#359 Desperate Passage
#360 Mission to Burma
#361 Final Resort
#362 Patriot Acts
#363 Face of Terror
#364 Hostile Odds
#365 Collision Course
#366 Pele's Fire
#367 Loose Cannon
#368 Crisis Nation
#369 Dangerous Tides
#370 Dark Alliance
#371 Fire Zone
#372 Lethal Compound
#373 Code of Honor
#374 System Corruption
#375 Salvador Strike
#376 Frontier Fury
#377 Desperate Cargo
#378 Death Run
#379 Deep Recon
#380 Silent Threat
#381 Killing Ground
#382 Threat Factor
#383 Raw Fury
#384 Cartel Clash

#385 Recovery Force
#386 Crucial Intercept
#387 Powder Burn
#388 Final Coup
#389 Deadly Command
#390 Toxic Terrain
#391 Enemy Agents
#392 Shadow Hunt
#393 Stand Down
#394 Trial by Fire
#395 Hazard Zone
#396 Fatal Combat
#397 Damage Radius
#398 Battle Cry
#399 Nuclear Storm
#400 Blind Justice
#401 Jungle Hunt
#402 Rebel Trade
#403 Line of Honor
#404 Final Judgment
#405 Lethal Diversion
#406 Survival Mission
#407 Throw Down
#408 Border Offensive
#409 Blood Vendetta
#410 Hostile Force
#411 Cold Fusion
#412 Night's Reckoning
#413 Double Cross
#414 Prison Code
#415 Ivory Wave
#416 Extraction
#417 Rogue Assault
#418 Viral Siege
#419 Sleeping Dragons
#420 Rebel Blast
#421 Hard Targets
#422 Nigeria Meltdown

The Executioner
Don Pendleton's ®

NIGERIA MELTDOWN

A GOLD EAGLE BOOK FROM

W⬥RLDWIDE ®

TORONTO • NEW YORK • LONDON
AMSTERDAM • PARIS • SYDNEY • HAMBURG
STOCKHOLM • ATHENS • TOKYO • MILAN
MADRID • WARSAW • BUDAPEST • AUCKLAND

Recycling programs
for this product may
not exist in your area.

First edition January 2014

ISBN-13: 978-0-373-64422-3

Special thanks and acknowledgment to
Andy Boot for his contribution to this work.

NIGERIA MELTDOWN

You must be the change you wish to see in the world.
—Mahatma Gandhi

I'm all for change if it has a positive effect. But I object to change forced to come about by the barrel of a gun.
—Mack Bolan

THE
MACK BOLAN
LEGEND

Nothing less than a war could have fashioned the destiny of the man called Mack Bolan. Bolan earned the Executioner title in the jungle hell of Vietnam.

But this soldier also wore another name—Sergeant Mercy. He was so tagged because of the compassion he showed to wounded comrades-in-arms and Vietnamese civilians.

Mack Bolan's second tour of duty ended prematurely when he was given emergency leave to return home and bury his family, victims of the Mob. Then he declared a one-man war against the Mafia.

He confronted the Families head-on from coast to coast, and soon a hope of victory began to appear. But Bolan had broken society's every rule. That same society started gunning for this elusive warrior—to no avail.

So Bolan was offered amnesty to work within the system against terrorism. This time, as an employee of Uncle Sam, Bolan became Colonel John Phoenix. With a command center at Stony Man Farm in Virginia, he and his new allies—Able Team and Phoenix Force—waged relentless war on a new adversary: the KGB.

But when his one true love, April Rose, died at the hands of the Soviet terror machine, Bolan severed all ties with Establishment authority.

Now, after a lengthy lone-wolf struggle and much soul-searching, the Executioner has agreed to enter an "arm's-length" alliance with his government once more, reserving the right to pursue personal missions in his Everlasting War.

1

He could hear them through the rain forest that clustered thickly about him. Even the chatter of birds and the rustle of animal life in the undergrowth around him could not deaden the sound of their calling. Anyone who was unfamiliar with the region would assume that they were hearing animal cries. Joseph Yobo was all too familiar with the region, so he knew that the sounds he heard could not come from an indigenous animal.

His enemy was communicating, and they were closing rapidly on him.

Sweat streamed from his forehead and into his eyes. He blinked and tried to wipe it away with either his forearm or what was left of his sleeve. The former was equally drenched in sweat and left behind as much as it removed; the latter was soaked in gasoline and stung horribly. In both cases, the salt of the sweat or the chemicals of the gasoline inflicted a direct, liquid and heated pain into the cuts that formed a jagged line across his forehead. The dripping perspiration of his brow was little more than an irritant compared to sudden agonies incurred by any attempt to remove it.

His chest ached and throbbed with a dull pain that was like a shard of glass left in the muscle to grind at the fibers. He had been weak when he had made his escape. Only the desperation and desire to stay alive and avoid a slow, painful death had given his feebled and battered body any kind of impetus. His legs were leaden, and his feet, he could no longer feel. Barefoot, cut to ribbons by the tortures he had been subjected to, he could not tell if there were any foreign bodies or infection in them.

He knew he was a dead man walking. Dead man stumbling, to be more accurate. His desire to keep moving meant that his upper body willed him forward faster than his shaking legs could manage, perpetually on the verge of tumbling onto his face. His willpower prevented that. Once down, he would not be able to rise, and then they would easily descend on him. While he was on his feet—even though his inability to retain complete control of his movements meant any subterfuge was doomed—he could still keep moving, making it just that much harder for them to pin him down.

Yobo had little doubt now that they would catch him before he reached the border. If he could reach Cameroon, he would be marginally safer. Even though the exact border between Cameroon and Nigeria was hidden by the rain forest of Cross River State, he knew that there was a village just into Cameroon where he could seek shelter. Celestine N'Joffi, a comrade from happier times—when Yobo had been seeking to graduate medical school as a military doctor—lived there. His was a small practice, but like many of the doctors in small villages and towns dotted around the highlands of Cameroon, it was doubtful if the settlements could maintain stability.

That had been especially true of the past few years, as the Brotherhood of the Eagle had soared over Nigeria and sought to spread its wings across the borders. Although the Yoruba-speaking men of Lagos chose to say little about the threat, the way in which it had pervaded the military culture of some sections, and the manner in which it had sought to finance itself, had been a thorn in the side of the government. Aware of the reputation that Nigeria had outside its borders for the widespread corruption within, this had been one such manifestation, which it had wanted to play down.

Joseph Yobo was an honorable man. When he had been taken from medical school during his last year—after being told that he could resume his studies when this mission was complete—and briefed on the secret mission that only he could undertake, as a man of integrity and new to the service, he had been only too pleased to serve the greater good.

Bitterly now, as acrid as the bile in his throat burning with every stumbling step, he knew that he had been set up to be betrayed from the beginning.

A root hidden in the damp soil caught on his foot. He didn't feel it as his ankle twisted, but by the way he fell, he knew that he had further injured the foot. Not that it mattered. His feet could never be saved, even if the rest of him somehow survived. They would need amputation—hopefully before the poisons in them spread through his bloodstream.

He had a more pressing problem: if the position of the sun was correct, as seen through the canopy of trees above him, then he was still three kilometers from the village, at the very least. He tried to haul himself to his feet, and the effort dragged every searing breath from his lungs. Lights flickered and burned bright before his eyes, his ears sang and his balance was disturbed by the feeling that he was about to lose consciousness. It was only the trunk of the very tree whose root had tripped him that enabled him to gain enough of a hold to keep himself upright.

Yobo moved forward on the bad ankle. It didn't hurt,

but by the same token, it gave way under him, pitching him forward. He swore. It would have been loudly, as the force of his anger had yanked it from his body, but his lack of strength rendered it as little more than a hoarse whisper. Still, it took him seconds to recover what little strength he had left. Seconds in which he could hear the sounds of alien animal cries as his pursuers gained ground.

How he wished that the engine on the old Mercedes truck had held for just a few kilometers more. He had rarely been able to get it out of second gear, and it had whined and bucked over the rough track that had been hacked from the terrain, but it had enabled him to make a head start as the sun had risen. How he had been able to muster the energy to loosen the leads on the other trucks, throwing them into the bush surrounding the camp, he did not know. It was all he had been able to do to take advantage of the one time that a lazy guard fell asleep on him. The Brotherhood guard had assumed Yobo had no strength and no fight left in him. He had been almost right about the former but never about the latter. Yobo had the flint-hard determination of a man who knew his own end was soon to come yet was determined that it would not be in vain. The man's own knife, slipped from its sheath while the fool slumbered, had taken his life before he had any inclination that things were wrong. His grunt of death could have been nothing more than a disturbance of his sleep.

With the sun still below the horizon, it had taken everything within Yobo to limp and stumble to the trucks and disable all but the one he would use. It had seen better days, but it appeared the best of a poor bunch. The engines had been covered in oil and gasoline, and he had smeared and ripped his sleeves as he disabled them. Cuts to his arms made no difference. The tattered camo pants and shirt that he had been given to cover himself after each torture session provided no warmth and protection. Their sole use to be in the humiliation that stripping him at the start of each session would cause.

Yobo was not a good driver, and that had cost him valuable time. He had no idea how much of a start he could really hope to expect—as long as it took them, once wakened by the sound of the ancient engine splitting the air, to discover who had escaped, and to recover and fit the leads he had taken from the remaining vehicles, he supposed. Even so, he knew that his lack of skill had reduced whatever chances he had and that rankled him.

His slow progress once on foot had not had the same effect. He had enough medical training to realize how badly debilitated he had been by his torture. Even when he had told them all that he knew, they had continued. First because they did not believe him and then for the sheer sport of seeing what further damage they could inflict.

They could not believe that General Oboko had sent him to infiltrate and report on the activities of the Brotherhood. Worse, whatever he reported was sure to be doctored before being passed onward and upward to Oboko's superiors, as the general was himself a member of the Brotherhood. His captors could not believe that Yobo had been so naive as to accept such a mission. But he was, and that was why the general had chosen him. That way Oboko could pay service to both sets of masters and keep himself on the right side of each.

Yobo felt like a fool. His payment for his naïveté would be his life, he knew that, but he would make sure that Oboko felt the wrath of any who may come after. Celestine would be able to help him. He had contacts outside Nigeria or Cameroon who would find this situation of interest. The Brotherhood was still a secret within Nigeria to a great degree, but even a fool like Joseph Yobo did not expect a complete blanket of silence to be without a few holes.

The coast was only a few kilometers away in the opposite direction. Port Harcourt, in the Rivers State, had been an area where he had spent some happy times with Abby. He knew he would never see her again. Knowing Oboko as he did, he had little doubt that the general had already made a point of personally calling to tell her that Yobo had been killed in the line of duty and offered her his own personal brand of consolation. Tears welled in his eyes when he thought of her face, but he realized that these were as much tears of self-pity that he would not see or touch her again as much as they were tears for what would happen to her. She would do what she had to in order to stay alive.

Gathering himself and sighting by the sun, Yobo blocked out the cries of those enemies closing in. There was nothing he could do about them. If they came upon him, then it was God's will that he would not live to tell.

God would provide some kind of salvation for him, he knew. Using his faith as a spur to dig deep within himself, Yobo began to hobble and hop painfully onward in the direction of the village that was his one remaining goal.

It would seem that God had deserted him in his hour of need. With howls of triumph, four men sprang from the undergrowth, pawing at him and dragging him to the ground. Speaking in Yoruba, one of them hissed in his ear that he would suffer before he died, so much so that he would be begging them to kill him.

He was wondering if he could suffer more, when a muted gunshot choked any further words in the man's throat, his eyes glazing and blood bubbling from his lips. Yobo was stunned. Could God have answered his pleas in a way that was too prosaic for him to understand?

A second shot sounded, and another of the men pitched

forward, a hole ripped in his chest by the exit wound, spraying the remaining two men and the prone Yobo with his viscera.

The pair of Brotherhood fighters were less brave and forthcoming when confronted with a sure-shot enemy that they could not see. Their bravado ebbed away to be replaced by panic as they looked around them, eyes wide with fear. Yobo lay pinned down by the corpse of the first man to be shot. He couldn't have managed to do much by way of escape, even if that had not been the case, but the two fighters left alive had forgotten him, shielded as he was by the dead man.

There were other animal calls and some shouts in Yoruba that gave away the panic of the men who made up the remainder of the separated Brotherhood pursuit party. Forgetting Yobo—perhaps to write him off as dead to their superiors if they should be questioned or indeed get out of the rain forest alive—the two warriors were less than fierce as they blundered noisily through the undergrowth, calling as they did. They were answered by bursts of gunfire that Yobo could identify as coming from Kalashnikovs—the Brotherhood weapon of choice, as the unit Yobo had been held by were holders of a large number of stolen AKs—which ripped into their own men as they approached.

For Joseph Yobo, there was a kind of irony in the fact that these pursuers were wiping each other out by sheer panic. In the camps and in training, they spoke of their courage at great length. Yet they had mostly been men from the northern territories, where the vast plains had no dense, enclosed jungle like the borders. Take them out of their comfort zones and they were reduced to panicking like schoolchildren.

That was the one thing he would wish to pass on to N'Joffi before he died. They were strong units within their own territories, but such was the nature of Nigeria that each region had its own geographic and tribal personality. Like many African nations, they had to contend with the contradictions thrown up by the arbitrary nature of the borders the old colonial nations had imposed on them.

Yobo's dry, cracked lips tried to smile. He was wandering in his thoughts, a sign that death was fast approaching him. It was a great shame that he had not been able to pass on any information, or even just to point the finger at that fat pig Oboko, who had lead him to his own death.

A grenade detonated about half a kilometer away. The impact, even at this distance, made the ground beneath him tremble, but he hardly noticed. Were the fools now throwing grenades at each other? Screams sounded in the aftermath: men in pain. The doctor in him pitied them. The victim in him wished them the same agonies that they had inflicted on him. He instantly regretted that. He was a good Christian, which was why it had been so easy for him to join the Brotherhood of the Eagle, and this spiritual belief made him feel shame at wishing ill on his pursuers. Although, of course, they too professed to be Christian but were quite happy to rape, pillage and murder any who crossed their path.

His smile turned into a choking, strangled laugh that degenerated into a cough that felt as though it would split his chest. Through the pain and his own hacking that filled his head, he was dimly aware that the cries and the gunfire had died down now. Into the gap came the sounds of the wildlife and birds, returning to their own existence, uninterrupted by man.

That was not all. He could hear the sound of one man, treading softly in the undergrowth. His footfalls had the lightness of a man familiar with the land, not a man who was hiding or seeking to evade detection. He even began to whistle, and Yobo recognized a Bhundu Boys' tune that he had grown up with. It filled him with a nostalgia and longing for what was left behind, while he still had breath to remember when life was good. Tears welled up and rolled down his cheeks, but he had not even the wherewithal to sob.

"Brotherhood scum. Let me see what I have stopped this time, count how many of you I have prevented from entering my beloved country."

The man's voice was distant in Yobo's receding consciousness but loud enough to be close. He tried to speak, but nothing came out. He heard the body of the man who had fallen close to him being turned over. Then he felt the body of the man on top of him being pulled off. Dimly he could see a tall, rangy man in camo vest and combat fatigues, a silenced SMG hanging from a strap on his shoulder, a pack over the other.

"What have we here? Lord, what were they doing to you, my son?" The hardness of his tone was replaced by a softer compassion, emphasized by the gentle French lilt to his voice. He leaned down and checked Yobo. "My God, what makes them do this to a man? How did you manage to come this far and evade them?"

Yobo tried to speak but couldn't. It was a miracle; it had to be. He recognized the man crouched over him. It was the man he had been seeking. Truly there had to be a God, albeit one who did not believe in making the lives of his believers easy.

2

Joseph Yobo had wanted to scream for the entire one-kilometer journey, like an eternity to him. Perception was a strange beast, as in truth Celestine N'Joffi had worked with the strength of ten to get his charge back to the village as quickly as possible. Even the brief examination in the forest had told him that there was very little chance he would be able to save Yobo's life. Yet if nothing else, he wished to make him comfortable for what little life he had left.

There had been no time for Celestine to go back to the village and get help; more than just that, he was loathe to leave Yobo alone and so unable to defend himself in the forest. Celestine was sure that he had driven away the last of the Brotherhood fighters, but that still left a lot of wildlife that would see a man in Yobo's condition as easy prey.

Quickly N'Joffi chopped down some branches with the panga he carried in a sheath on his thigh, then used strips of cloth to augment and strengthen the vine and bark that he fashioned into a makeshift stretcher. Once he had done that, sweat and effort sticking his vest to his body, he gently lifted Yobo onto the pallet.

With no little regret in his voice, he said, "This will hurt, my friend. I cannot lie to you. But if I am to get you to my clinic quickly, there is no other way. Courage, Joseph, and I will give you morphine when we get there. The pain will deaden soon enough then."

Breathing heavily, he took the weight of the stretcher and pulled it along the path that he had fashioned in the forest, leading back to his village. It was a path that could not be seen unless you knew what you were looking for, such was his skill in building it. He had made many like this since the Brotherhood had started to encroach on the borderlands, enabling him to cross the forest with ease. It was rougher still with a sick and dying man at your back, knowing that every bump and jolt was agony to him, but it was as swift as was possible.

When Celestine was a short distance from the village, and still camouflaged by the forest, he called out in a series of soft sighs and clicks. The signal brought forth three armed men who looked at him askance. He said simply, "Friend." Such was the trust they held in N'Joffi that they did not hesitate to assist him in taking the prone man to his cabin, even though he appeared to be one of the hated and feared Brotherhood. His injuries showed he was no threat, but everyone in the village had suffered at the hands of the Brotherhood, and a man of Yobo's appearance would normally be cut down without question.

Having sent his assistants to continue the patrol he had started, N'Joffi made Yobo as comfortable as possible on one of the medical beds in his cabin and prepared a shot of morphine. As he injected it, he took in his old friend at a glance. Even without a proper examination, he didn't give much for Yobo's chances of survival. Certainly his feet were gangrenous and would need amputation—he had no way of knowing that Yobo had already accepted that—but it was doubtful that he had the resources out here to complete such an operation successfully.

"Quiet, Joseph. Rest now. I will try to make you as

comfortable as possible," N'Joffi said softly as Yobo continued striving to speak.

He had something to say that he felt was of great importance, but if he did not rest, then he would never be able to say it. As it was, N'Joffi was almost certain that whatever it might be would be Yobo's closing statement to the world.

That impression was only enhanced by the work he put into tending Yobo's wounds. The man had been tortured repeatedly over a long period, and many of the older wounds had festered. In this climate, it did not take long for infection to set in. Add that to the actual injuries themselves, and it was astounding to the doctor that his patient had even made it this far.

Almost as astounding, in truth, as stumbling across an old friend in the middle of a jungle, thousands of miles from where they had last met.

Like Yobo, N'Joffi was a believer in God and the ways in which He moved the lives of men. Unlike his friend, N'Joffi was not so much of a wide-eyed innocent. Even before he had opted to come to this outpost and set up practice, he had been wiser to the ways of men. His work outside medicine had given him that perspective. He had a feeling that the contacts he had picked up along the way would also soon be of use to him.

He kept watch over Yobo while he slept. He did not want him to die yet. Partly because of what he was so desperate to impart. Why was a trainee military doctor so far from where he had last been based? From what he knew of Yobo, N'Joffi suspected that the Brotherhood would be anathema to Yobo. So why did he seem to have been one of them and yet also treated in such a manner? It was not too great a leap of imagination to surmise that he had been an agent of some kind, and that he had arrived in this place—in desperate flight—because he knew that he might find shelter. After all, N'Joffi could recall Yobo's shock that N'Joffi would wish to bury himself so far from the city life he loved.

That gave N'Joffi a greater sense of responsibility. He had been the last hope of this shattered shell of a man. He could not let Yobo down at the last.

That night was crucial, not just to see if Yobo could survive until daybreak, but because the information he was about to give would alter the course of history in Nigeria, even if this would only ever be known to a privileged few. N'Joffi nursed him closely, making him as comfortable as possible and allowing him as much rest as would restore what was left of his strength.

When dawn broke, Yobo was able to sit upright and drink some fluids without vomiting them immediately. A weak grin suffused his features, but he was not fooled. He knew this surge of strength would not last.

"Do not lie to me," he croaked in a harsh whisper. "How long do you think I have?"

"Maybe a day or two," N'Joffi replied without hesitation. The verdict was harsh but tempered by the compassion in his voice. He knew Yobo well enough to not treat him like a fool.

"Then it is necessary that I tell you all I know, so that you may pass it on to someone who will be able to smash this filth in my country."

"Our country," N'Joffi interjected. Although he came from—and now lived—in the south of Cameroon, the region had been part of Nigeria until fifty years past. There were some who wished it had never changed. N'Joffi was one of those.

Yobo nodded slowly. "It is true, my friend. I may not be able to tell you all I know more than once. I will recall as much detail as I can. It may be best to record it in some way."

N'Joffi had already thought of that. His cell phone had all the capacity he would need, and he set it to recording while Yobo began his story. It was long and rambling, and he had to break off several times to cough and hack painfully. N'Joffi gave him glucose solutions to help, but most times the liquid came straight back up in a pained, broken stream. It was only the man's willpower that drove him on.

With more than an hour of details on the SIM card of the cell phone, an exhausted Yobo leaned back, his eyes closing.

"I have done what I can. This is what happened to me, Celestine. It must not happen to anyone else. These people must be stopped. How many more men like Oboko—" he spit the name with a venom that sapped him of what little strength remained "—are there in the military, poisoning it and making our nation weak?"

N'Joffi looked at his cell phone, and then at his dying friend. What he had heard—what he had as a record—was explosive. It provided a key to the heart of the organization that was like a cancer in the country. Yet who could he take it to? Within Nigeria, it could not be assumed that any institution or individual was safe. Even if the physician found an honest and true man, he would be surrounded by the corrupt. In Cameroon, although the levels of corruption were nowhere near as high as in Nigeria, there was still the suspicion that the Brotherhood had ears that could hear.

There was one man he could trust, but he was not on this continent. N'Joffi would have to make sure that this man got to hear what he had recorded. This should be simple enough in terms of technology.

But otherwise? The Brotherhood might still be looking for Yobo. Its militia, which had been trying to infiltrate the border area for some months, was camped deep in the forest and hard to root out. Their incursions across the border had been repelled so far, because they were not as familiar with the landscape as the people who had lived here for generations.

That balance in favor of the locals was shifting away as the superior firepower and military training of the Brotherhood fighters was beginning to tell. The villagers were farmers and fishermen, not soldiers. Their weapons were few. Their desire to fight was less. N'Joffi could see the village being overrun within a few months, unless things changed, and there would be no place for him then. He would have to leave or else face a certain death for his opposition.

The Brotherhood had not sent men for Yobo during the night. This was a good sign. They were still adjusting to the territory, as the ease with which Celestine had scattered them on the previous day could prove. But now it was morning, and they had more confidence. If he was lucky, they would not want to admit their failure to their leaders and would report that Yobo had been killed. Maybe they even believed that.

N'Joffi could take no chances. He had become de facto leader of the village by reason of his knowledge of military tactics, gleaned from his stay in Lagos and his training as a military doctor. The nominal head of the village deferred to him and trusted his instincts.

"Rest now, Joseph. I must go and see that we are well protected. Do not worry, my friend, I know what I can do with your story. We will stop these people."

Yobo stayed him with a feeble grip as he turned to exit. "My friend, first take a moment to pray with me."

N'Joffi nodded solemnly and knelt beside Yobo's bed.

The two men prayed together before Yobo patted his friend on the hand.

"Go and do what you must, now."

N'Joffi rose and left him, his heart sinking as he went out of the cabin and toward the cantina that was used as a meeting place for the village's defense force. There were a few men waiting for him, expectant for their day's orders. N'Joffi organized the patrols that would keep the village safe and sent them on their way before returning to his cabin.

He was saddened, but not surprised, to find that Joseph Yobo had died while he was away. His wish was to give his friend a good Christian burial, but he could not do that. Joseph would understand why.

ABBY KOSOKO FELT that she was lucky to live in Lagos, in the Ogun region of south Nigeria. As she walked home from church, she reflected that the northern part of the country was becoming a dangerous place for anyone with Christian values. The Muslims were taking a greater hold, and there was talk that English and Common Law—under which Nigeria had worked for so long—was being abolished in favor of Sharia Law, even though the government had long since decreed such a thing could not happen.

Like many in her part of the world, she was immune to the idea that there may be reasonable people in other religions, dismissing them as radicals. By the same token, she had not believed Joseph when he had spoken to her of radical Christians who sought to overthrow the present regime in the same way as the radical Islamists sought to in the north. She felt the idea of the radical north being suppressed was a good thing. When he had posited the idea that a radical Christian south would be equally as bad and against the teachings of the Bible, she had disagreed with him.

Now he was gone. He had told her that he was being sent on a mission that would prove the veracity of what he had said. She had believed that, in truth, he was doing little more than going on maneuvers for the military part of his training, and would soon return to her and take up his medical studies again.

But as time had gone on, and she had heard nothing from him, she had started to worry. Perhaps he had been telling the truth? If that was so, she would owe him an apology. She had wanted them to be married. He had wanted to wait until his training was complete. She would, perhaps, insist that she get her own way. She always did eventually.

These thoughts occupied her mind, and she did not notice the Ford sedan waiting outside her house. It was only when the guttural voice of General Franklin Oboko called to her that she realized how caught up in her own world she had been. She turned to see the general heaving his vast bulk from the rear of the vehicle.

"Abby! What is wrong with you, child? You are deaf all of a sudden?"

"I'm sorry, General. I was lost in thought," she answered as he left the chauffeur-driven state car and rolled toward her.

Oboko was a huge man: over six feet and almost 280 pounds, squeezed into a uniform that was stained with the same heavy sweat that he mopped from his forehead in the early afternoon heat.

"You must call me Franklin, I keep telling you," he said, ushering her toward her front door while his chauffeur averted his eyes as the general's hand patted her buttocks.

"I wasn't expecting you— Have you had word of Joseph?" she asked as Oboko closed the door behind them.

Abby lived with her mother, but at this time of day, she was out working. Oboko would know that.

"Abby, you must sit down. I must talk to you and it is not good," Oboko said flatly. He was not renowned for his tact. The bewildered young woman sat, thoughts crowding into her mind. The tone of the general's voice, and the fact that he was calling unexpectedly, could only mean one thing.

He continued, with his usual lack of subtlety. "You know that it was a very dangerous mission that I sent Joseph on. I would not have trusted anyone else, but even so, it was very unlikely that he would come back. I have to say that I was right in that. I have had word that he has been brutally killed. But you must not be sorry, my dear, because he died like a hero."

She opened her mouth to speak but started to sob.

Oboko moved and put his arm around her. "You are upset. Of course I will comfort you...."

She tried to resist, but the general was more than twice her weight and a good foot taller. She had little chance of stopping him, as he forced himself on her, muttering in her ear that she would feel better, and that a real man would show her that she wasn't missing much with Joseph gone.

"I will come and see how you are on Friday," he said as he adjusted his uniform, leaving her on the sofa blank eyed and numbed. "You will say nothing of this to your mother, of course. That would not be a wise thing to do. For your mother," he added, considering that she was nearer his age, but still a fine-looking woman for all that.

Abby shook her head but could not look at the general as he left her.

Outside he wiped the sweat from his forehead and heaved himself into the back of the sedan, barking an order at his driver to return to headquarters.

He had satisfied the government. He had satisfied his

Brotherhood paymasters. And now he had satisfied himself, with the promise of more to come.

Life was good. What could possibly go wrong?

3

Adam Mars-Jones left the chamber and walked back to his office deep in thought. It had been a vigorous debate, the deep divisions caused by religious and tribal rivalries in the region making for entrenched viewpoints that had baffled the South American and European delegates.

He had been appointed America's delegate to the UN group because of his family background—his parents were of Nigerian and Cameroon origins, though he had been born in San Francisco—and because of the work he had undertaken in the two countries since joining the UN after graduation. It had to be said that even he found the intransigence of some parties both frustrating and confusing.

As he walked through the antechamber to his office, his secretary caught the glower on his face and elected to wait until he was behind closed doors before letting him know about the request.

"What the hell could he want?" Mars-Jones growled when informed via the intercom. "I'm not really in the mood—"

"He was most insistent about its importance," she told him. "Most insistent," she repeated.

Mars-Jones sighed. "Okay, try to set it up for me, will you? I'll get my own coffee while you do it." He hated Skype conversations at the best of times, the lag in some of the relay meaning that he could easily misjudge someone's mood. He also had a thing about technology and didn't even have an MP3 player, though he was loathe to admit that in front of anyone. He was happier with his secretary setting up the call for him.

By the time he had downed one cup of coffee and poured another to take back to his desk, his monitor showed the Skype conference call in setup. Within a few seconds, Dr. Celestine N'Joffi's face appeared on the screen.

Mars-Jones's mild displeasure and irritation vanished as he caught the Cameroonian's expression. "Celestine, this must be important," he said without preamble.

"It is," N'Joffi replied earnestly. He could see on his laptop that Mars-Jones looked tired and distracted. "This may not be a good time for you—"

"It isn't, if I'm honest. I would have rescheduled or put you off if you hadn't been so insistent to my secretary. But now that I can see you—"

"Good. I would not risk such a communication, with no security, unless it was a matter of time."

Mars-Jones leaned forward. It was a long way from his air-conditioned office in New York to the sweltering heat of a Cameroon village, but his attention was so intent that he might as well have been in the same room. He listened in silence while N'Joffi briefly outlined the situation as it stood in the jungle along the border.

"Sorry to interrupt," Mars-Jones interjected, "but what is the Brotherhood of the Eagle, and why—"

"Haven't you heard anything about the Brotherhood in the U.S.?" N'Joffi asked, taken aback.

When Mars-Jones shook his head, N'Joffi laughed harshly. "The government and military do not want this getting out, but it is growing and for the most part from within. Let me tell you something—the way that the Muslims in the north have taken hold is causing a backlash that the Brotherhood of the Eagle is taking advantage of. I do not care about Islam as long as it does not care about me. They are mostly like that, but in the south, the people do not think of that. They go to church, and they do not think of God. They only think about the gap between Christians and Muslims. They are scared, and they respond to anyone who says they are Christian and will drive out unbelievers.

"They recruit and brainwash, then they go out and kill for control, cash and food. And they are growing in power. They have men inside the military and the government, and this is what keeps the noise down."

"Okay, let's leave the religion out of this," Mars-Jones said carefully.

N'Joffi glared at him. "I know why you say that, and you are right in America, but not here."

Mars-Jones nodded. "I get it. What exactly is it that makes you call me now?"

"You know where I am. We have had a large amount of paramilitary activity as the Brotherhood tries to come into this country. It has been of some concern, and once the Cameroon regime get nervous, then I think the world will hear a loud noise. Two days ago I was on patrol…"

Settling into his story, now more concise as he had to relay facts and not explain that which, to his frustration, he felt Mars-Jones should know, N'Joffi told of discovering Yobo, taking him back to the village and tending him until he died.

"Before he passed, while he still had strength, he made me record all that he had discovered. It needs action, and you are the only man I can think of. I will play it for you now, but I have already compressed the file and sent it to you by email so that you have a copy. First, I had to speak to you, to impress its importance on you. Please, listen…"

Mars-Jones agreed and sat in silence while N'Joffi held up his cell phone to the webcam on the laptop and played back Joseph Yobo's statement. He could see the Cameroonian's eyes well up as he heard his dead friend's voice again.

When the recording had finished, N'Joffi switched off his cell phone and set it in front of him. He stared into the webcam, momentarily unable to speak. Finally, he said, "Joseph Yobo was a good man. He undertook a mission in good faith, for the right reasons, and was treated like a goat tethered for a lion. He deserved better. The people of these lands deserve better. I know that you have contacts. Perhaps it is time for you to use them."

Mars-Jones was silent for a moment then he nodded decisively.

"Celestine, my old friend, I know just the man. Believe me, this will be sorted, no matter the cost."

WHEN OBOKO GOT to the barracks, he walked across the parade ground to his office with a sense of satisfaction that caused a lascivious grin to spread across his face as he recalled the previous hour. He had time to reflect on his conquest, as the military headquarters on the edge of Lagos was a large barracks, housing several troop divisions as well as administrative buildings, and the largest drill and parade ground in the region. It was an active base, and although Oboko also had an office in the defense office located in the center of the city, he found that the bureaucrats and desk soldiers who manned the building were more circumspect and also more cunning that he was. Oboko had too much he wanted kept dark to risk falling into their hands.

The general crashed open the door of his office, allowed himself a full-throated chuckle as he recalled Abby's face and pulled open a drawer of the nearby filing cabinet. He removed a bottle of cane rum brewed in an illegal still in the barracks and took a slug straight from the bottle before slamming it back into the drawer.

Then he turned toward his desk and realized he was not alone.

"You are a satisfied man, Oboko," his unwelcome visitor said in a menacingly quiet undertone.

"Milton! I was not expecting you," Oboko blustered. "Did you arrange this with my adjutant? That man is a fool—"

"Shut up, Franklin," Major Milton Abiola whispered in the same tone. He was seated behind Oboko's desk, and he gestured with the swish cane he held that the general take the subordinate position. As their military rank and standing mattered little when the two men were in private, Oboko did as he was told without any dissent.

"Why have you come to see me?" Oboko asked in a small, scared voice.

"You have good reason to speak like that," Abiola replied. His face was dark with anger, the scars on his cheeks more livid, making his face immobile but only accentuating the anger that burned in his eyes. "Joseph Yobo—"

"Has been dealt with. You know that the men—"

"They say. I know nothing for certain, and this worries me. I want his body, so that I can see with my own eyes that he is really dead."

"It is done. Look, let me show you." Oboko hefted his bulk out of the chair. It was old, unsteady and designed to make whoever sat in it facing the general feel uneasy. It was certainly working on the general himself right now. He came around so that he was standing over Abiola. Cursing, he tried to get his PC working, banging the mouse down and swearing under his breath when the machine froze. Abiola watched him with a sneer curling on his lip.

"Look, you see? It is done," Oboko finally said triumphantly when he managed to get the technology to obey him. Opening his email, he clicked on one with an attachment: a piece of video ran, showing two men in camouflage clothing kneeling by a body that had been mauled, but was still readily identifiable as that of Yobo. "We finished him."

"You finished him and then let the jackal eat him before taking pictures?" Abiola scoffed.

"There was an unfortunate incident," Oboko spluttered. "In the forest there was confusion, and some of the men fired on others by mistake. The men with Yobo were killed, and it took some time—"

"You are a fool, and you think I am as stupid as you?" Abiola asked softly. "You do not know for certain what happened any more than I do. That is an unsafe region for us. If the Cameroon government gets to know what we are doing before we have sweetened them—"

"No one knows anything," Oboko said, panicked and hurried. He held up his hands. "I have this film, sent anonymously to me, which I will show my superior officer as proof that our mission to infiltrate the Brotherhood was not a success. It is regrettable, but—"

Abiola pushed back his chair and rose. He was several inches shorter than the general and about eighty pounds lighter, being a lean and muscular man, but even so he had a bearing that made the general quail and shrink before him.

"You are more than a fool. We cannot let the world see what we are doing. We cannot let our government see— at least, not those we do not already own. Let me tell you something, Franklin. When I was a boy, my father told me tales about Biafra, and how the government crushed the people and made them conform. The world protested, but we starved them until they were forced to give in. We showed them no mercy, because they were the start of a domino crash that would have seen good Christian men fall beneath the Communist heel." He brought the swish cane down on the desk with a loud crack that made Oboko wince.

"If we do not act now, generations later, the same will happen in the northern regions, but it will be the Islamist heel, not that of the godless, that will seek to crush us. Forty years ago we had only a few to crush. Now they are sweeping across the continent. They must be stopped."

Milton Abiola had the faraway look in his eye of a zealot. Franklin Oboko was more concerned with the smaller things. What he had done with Abby and the bottle in the filing cabinet: those things would not be so easy with another kind of regime.

"Joseph Yobo was a good spy. Better than I thought, or I would not have picked him. But even the best spy has to tell someone his secrets, and Yobo was dead before he had chance, Milton. Trust me."

BENJAMIN WILLIAMS WAS a man who remembered Biafra but for very different reasons than Milton Abiola's. He was a man who sweated as heavily as Franklin Oboko, but again for a very different reason. As a young man, Williams had been a Nigerian soldier who had fought in the Biafran war, and the memory of those bowel-shattering days when he did not know if each second would be his last had never left him.

Fear and caution had dogged his every move since then, and this was why he was one of the most moderate of politicians on the African continent. Fear was what made him sweat now, as he sat before Adam Mars-Jones—who was familiar to him—and the heavyset American—who was unfamiliar to him. Even in the dark blue suit, he may well have looked like an administrator, but his bearing spoke of a past that was anything but deskbound.

"Adam, you are a good man, but you know that there are certain things within my country that must remain here. We are not in a stable position, and any upset could cause a ripple that—"

"Sir," the heavyset man said, leaning forward as he interjected, "I will be blunt with you, if I may. Mr. Mars-Jones is acquainted with me, and he knows the kind of matters that pass through my hands. He has some knowledge of your country and has briefed me as much as possible. I am aware of the restrictions under which you may operate, but at the same time, would urge you to speak freely within these walls, so that we may find a strategy to help you and your government—or at least, those elements of it with which you, and we, may be in sympathy."

Williams blew his nose loudly then mopped at his forehead with the same handkerchief. He studied both men hard before beginning.

"You know, since the British gave us independence, we have struggled with what they left behind. We have three types of law in the land. One based on what they left us, one based on our forefathers and one which has come in with the advent of Islam. I have no beef with Muslims. I will live alongside them as long as they do not bear us ill will. But adding their law to those we already have… it causes confusion, my friend, and that is what we have. But there is more. The British administrators given to us by the empire were lazy and greedy men, and they did everything according to what they could make from it. Very well, that was their choice. But the trouble has come since they left, because those they taught to run our administration—their administration—also learned their ways, and over the generations we have grown lazy and used to those ways."

"You mean that you run your country on corruption and money?" The American shrugged. "Most countries run that way to a greater or lesser extent."

Williams smiled sadly. "Not like Nigeria, my friend. It is a joke in some countries and even among my own countrymen. They are right, sadly. But this is a problem, as it is easy to buy silence and a blind eye. Simple, too, to keep things quiet that you would not want known."

"The Brotherhood of the Eagle," Mars-Jones said. "I have played for Mr. Brognola the recording sent to me, just as I have played it to you."

Williams shook his head. "It saddens me, but it does not surprise me."

"Are you trying to tell me that you didn't know about this?" the big Fed asked, genuinely surprised. There was something about Williams's tone of resignation that shocked him. "You're an ambassador—surely you're in touch with what happens in your own country?"

"Is anyone who spends so long away?" Williams countered. "Especially if you want to continue… Does that not give you a kind of distance?"

Brognola shrugged. "I guess. What do you know?"

"I know that there are many in my government who are scared of Islam, and what the wave of insurrection across the Arab lands and down the African continent could mean. I know there are many who are scared because they are Christian, and they fear the ones they think of as godless. I know there are many who feel that it is time that the Yoruba speakers and their beliefs took the control they have long believed their right. And I know that many of the people in these groups are the same men. But they have learned to keep their views to themselves. They meet in secret and make their plans. Some of them have decided to go further, and they wish to make these plans real."

"This is what the Brotherhood is?" Brognola prompted.

"In part. The British gave us many things, including their wonderful freemasonry. In my country, it has become debased, and the fact that it is secret and with rituals fits very well with many of our traditions. I know that the Brotherhood of the Eagle has adopted many of its methods to ensure that those who join are sworn to secrecy on pain of death and know that this would be the case. They hide themselves and know only by secret signs who their fellows may be. If you do not know the signs, then you cannot tell."

"Will you help me get inside the government and inside the Brotherhood?" Brognola asked.

"How? How can I do that when I do not know who is one of them and who is not?" Williams asked, shrugging helplessly.

"Do you have one man who you can trust implicitly who is in a position of some power?" the big Fed asked.

Williams did not hesitate. "I have one man. Only one man. But I would trust him with my life. I have in the past, and I am still here."

Brognola grinned. "I'll take your word on that, sir. As long as you have one, that's all I need. One man is all it will take, on both sides," he added, leaving Williams and Mars-Jones looking a little puzzled. "Trust me."

THE FIRST BUILDING was empty. The advance party had laid motion detectors there, when the patrols had passed. Symons and Prentiss were back with the team now, activating the tech so that they could keep track. If anyone tried to access the building during maneuvers, then they would automatically be informed.

Three hundred yards from the first building lay the second and third. Like the first, they were made of adobe and rock, hewn directly from the ground and fashioned into a dwelling, just as buildings like them had been for thousands of years.

The Taliban hadn't existed thousands of years ago; it had been a little more peaceful then. Now the insurgents were driving forward and taking territory while the UN forces had to withdraw. As the so-called rebels drove on, they were subjecting the populations they overran to their own version of justice.

Mack Bolan, aka the Executioner, couldn't remember ever reading the parts of a holy book that said you stoned people to death for dancing or gathering together. That wasn't freedom by anyone's definition. That was why the UN was here, to stop it from happening.

Bolan was here, heading up this five-man team, because a minor royal from a European house was also a serving marine, and in the course of doing his duty, he had found himself targeted by the Taliban, a small faction of which had decided that a plan to behead the royal and his bodyguard, to be filmed and uploaded to the YouTube website, might just cause a whole load of embarrassment.

So it would. That was why the President of the United States had personally requested that the soldier step in. He was the man for the job, and he was discreet.

Recon had told him that the royal and his bodyguard were kept in the farthest building, shackled and under armed guard by three men. There were three others in the closest building who were resting while their comrades took watch. Two men were on foot patrol. They had been watched for three circuits and timed. They were now at the optimum distance for the attack force to move.

The landscape was flat and arid. In the distance, low hills rose, goats rested for the night. There were no other dwellings, no other people, in hearing or sight. The Taliban faction had deliberately chosen the location. If they'd sent Bolan a text message asking him what he wanted, they couldn't have done better.

Bolan detailed Symons and Prentiss to keep the base secured. Hillier was the senior officer on the mission, and to him Bolan entrusted the advance. He was to scout the area around the far building and act as watch. While he did that, Bolan and Frewin, a saturnine marine with few words but the eyes of a man who had seen much, would take the secondary building and eliminate the sleeping Taliban. They were outnumbered three to two, so they would need speed to gain the advantage.

Hillier moved off at Bolan's prompting, and they gave him a two-minute start. Frewin watched through his night vision monocle, grunting when Hillier reached the first of the occupied buildings.

Following the soldier's lead, Frewin followed as they tracked in Hillier's wake, their earpieces alert to any word of change from base. It was clear: the patrol was nowhere near.

While Hillier established watch on the second target building, Bolan and Frewin took in the first. There was only one doorway and two windows that were covered with plastic sheeting, which would probably make a noise when cut. They couldn't afford to rouse those inside. Bolan took a chance and tried the door; it gave easily. Three shapes huddled on the floor, covered in blankets.

Nodding to Frewin, the Executioner drew the Gillette stainless-steel knife that he had honed earlier in the day.

The marine did likewise. They moved inside and took the two nearer figures, bending and executing them each with a simple clinical stroke. The third man was awakened by the faint sound and was rising, his mouth open to cry out, when Frewin's boot caught him in the face, strangling any cry at birth. The marine followed the blow by pinning the man and finishing the job.

Bolan and Frewin moved toward the main target. Hillier saw them approach through his monocle, reporting in a whisper into his mic.

"Objectives one and two on the left hand from the door, far wall. Targets at seven o'clock and eleven o'clock."

"Launch cover now," Bolan replied.

As Hillier fired a smoke grenade through the sheeted window, Bolan and Frewin slipped masks into place and broke into a run, taking the door with a crash, one man turning to each side. The confusion generated by the smoke had slowed the Taliban fighters' reactions. Short bursts from the infiltrators' machine pistols took out the two guards before they had a chance to recover.

Bolan and Frewin took a shackled man each and pulled them through the choking smoke. As they did, they heard an exchange of fire cut the night air. Looking across quickly, Bolan could see that Hillier had taken out the two foot patrol guards as they rushed back toward the buildings.

The solider took the gag and blindfold from the royal and his guard.

"Can you walk?" he asked them, indicating their shackles.

"More like hobble, but bloody quick," the royal replied with a grin. "Just show me the way so I can get these cut off."

"We have two men with tools a few hundred yards out," Bolan replied.

"Thanks… That was a bloody good show," the royal said as they started to move. He indicated his bodyguard. "I think we could both learn a bit from you lads."

4

"I hope you enjoy your stay with us, Mr. Cooper, and that it proves to be a productive visit."

The customs officer grinned broadly as he closed Bolan's case, returned the passport and visa in the name of Matthew Cooper and slipped the buff envelope into his hip pocket. It contained three hundred USD and had been advised as the best way for any businessman to get through customs and into Lagos without any undue worries. And so it had. Bolan figured that if this was any kind of indication, then it was going to be one hell of a trip. Frankly he would be relieved as soon as he could get away from so-called civilization and out into the field.

It would have suited him better if he could have come straight from Afghanistan, with Stony Man forwarding the relevant papers to a military base along the way and a phone call briefing from Hal. But the big Fed had determined that it would be better if he returned to the U.S. and met with Benjamin Williams and Adam Mars-Jones face-to-face.

The prospect of some serious jet lag on the round-trip journey from the east to the west and back again had not put him in the best of moods. This was something that had hardly been improved by hearing from Williams about the state of Nigeria and the problems within its borders. In truth, negotiating his way around the issues struck him as something that was better suited to a diplomat who could fire a gun rather than a soldier.

It was only when Mars-Jones had made his point that Mack's view had changed. "Mr. Cooper, at present the whole continent of Africa is in flux. It is not just about religions, it is about the political ideologies that are attached to those religions. If the unrest that is sweeping across the Arabic regions of Africa comes toward the south, it could set off a tidal wave of disturbances that would engulf the continent as a whole, and set up conditions for power struggles that could affect Europe, the Americas and even spread across the states of the old USSR. Vast political bases could change. The world could change and probably not for the best."

In a time of economic upheaval and turmoil, there was always a political flux and the chance of a sudden void being filled by something that used hate and fear to achieve its ends. This was what had blighted the middle of the twentieth century. Could it happen again?

"Why is taking on the Brotherhood of the Eagle so important?" he had asked. "Are you telling me that they're Christian? Then by your terms, they'd be up against the forces you see as destabilizing."

"They say they are Christian and perhaps they are," Mars-Jones mused. "Or perhaps they have an agenda that we have not, as yet, quite worked out. Our informant discovered that they have men in the Muslim factions in north Nigeria. Whether these men are spies, or whether they have some other function…"

The unknown enemy was always more dangerous, simply for that reason. There was no time to work out their motives; there was only time to root them out and destroy them.

That was why Matt Cooper, representative of a U.S. chemical corporation negotiating a lucrative contract for pesticides with the Nigerian government, had landed at Murtala Muhammed International near Lagos with a letter in his billfold arranging a meeting with Wole Achebe, the minister for agriculture.

The airport was crowded and hot, despite the air-conditioning that was running full blast.

Exiting the building, the only real difference was the heat that hit like a wall of fire as Bolan stepped out into the middle of the day. There were several cab drivers vying for his attention, and as soon as he had calmed them down enough to actually get into a cab and issue his destination, he was being assailed by a hail of questions from his driver. How long was he staying, what was he doing, did he need a guide, was this his first time here, if he was meeting the minister then he had to be an important—rich—man, and he would need a driver for his stay, wouldn't he? All of the questions were delivered as one stream, without much pause for Bolan to answer, even if he had been inclined.

His head began to throb in time with the deep funk beat of the old Fela Kuti track thumping from the antique cassette player wired into the battered cab. It was a song from the days when the singer was beaten by the then-regime, and to even listen to him marked you down as a dissident. The military had ruled the country with an iron fist in those years. Looking at the driver in his own rear-view mirror, Bolan could see that he was lined and scarred, showing years of hard life.

"You have to have a lion's heart to live in this country, I hear," he said, breaking across the man's stream of questions. "Only if you do, can you have the wings of an eagle and soar free."

The driver stopped dead in the middle of his monologue

and studied his passenger shrewdly in the rearview mirror, his eyes off the road but never deviating in his swerving path between the cars, motorbikes and pedestrians with little to do but follow their own individual sets of rules.

"That is a very strange thing to say, my friend," the driver murmured in a surprisingly soft voice. "Have you been here before?"

Bolan inclined his head. "No, but you hear things. Word gets out."

The driver leaned forward and switched off the cassette player. "You should be very careful how you speak. I remember a time when the military ruled this land, and a man could die for saying the wrong thing."

"And now?"

"A man can still die for saying the wrong thing. If you wish to play with the Brotherhood of the Eagle, be aware that they take their games as seriously as life and death, my friend. You are a businessman, yes?"

"I'm here on business," Bolan replied in a circumspect manner.

"Then you know that in order to get business done, it is necessary to be careful about what you say and who you speak to."

"I do. But I also know that there are people you can talk to, and you don't always have to question them first. You just need to be able to read the signs."

He saw in the rearview mirror the cab driver break a crooked grin. "You are a smart man, and I think you are in more than one kind of business. Forget all that I asked you before. I ask you just the one question. But not yet. Look first out the back window and tell me what you see."

As much as the narrow seat and slitted back window of the cab would allow, Bolan did as he was asked. Weaving through traffic, he could see four young men on motorbikes. They were keeping an equal distance from the cab, never coming any closer despite gaps in the flow that would allow them to speed past.

"Muggers," the cab driver said. "They like to come through the traffic and attack tourists. Usually, they come for those stupid enough to leave windows open, which most do in the heat. You haven't. I wonder if they are expecting you. You know, I once had a woman in my cab—a black British woman—whose family came from here. She had come back to find her roots. She found they were not here— She did not listen to me and was stupid enough to put a camcorder out the window and have it snatched from her hand. They nearly broke her wrist. I think she soon got a flight back to London. Do you think you were expected?"

"I shouldn't be. How about we turn the tables, ask them a few questions?"

The cab driver chuckled. "You are mad, my friend. I might be setting you up...but then, I think you are confident you could take me down, too."

"Let's not put it to the test," Bolan replied.

Another chuckle was his only answer before he was thrown across the seat by a sudden maneuver.

Swerving across the traffic and raising a cloud of dust from the dirt that swirled in the air then settled on the tarmac, the battered cab turned sharply on the corner of a side street, cutting across traffic that also screeched as straining brakes tried to prevent a collision. No vehicles hit the cab, which scattered pedestrians in its path, yelling and cursing. However, the taxi smashed a fruit stall with its tight turn. Some people threw the bouncing produce at the retreating car for hire. In its wake, those vehicles that had avoided a collision from the front were not so lucky from the rear, as those behind them failed to halt in time, careering into their back ends with a crunch of metal, a cacophony of broken glass and angry voices. Police whistles sounded as the military and civilian police rushed to stop the fights that were breaking out.

Under normal circumstances, it might have been expected that the chaos would also halt the bikers in their tracks. These were not normal circumstances, nor were they normal bikers. They were used to chaos—in truth, were usually the ones responsible for its cause—and so ignored the traffic and milling crowds, weaving between the two and kicking away those who strayed too close. It took them longer than they would have liked to navigate a path through the locked-together tangle of metal that was the traffic around the corner, but as they grouped together to take the turn and head down the road, they could see ahead of them that the cab had slowed, its brake lights glowing, as it waited for them to come in sight.

The four bikers exchanged glances. They had realized their mark had caught on to their plan, but could not fathom why, in that case, the cab would want them to catch up. All they knew was that they had a mission.

Bolan looked out the back window and saw them cluster at the head of the street. "Are you armed?" he asked the cab driver.

"I would be foolish if I was not, on these streets," the cab driver said with a grin. "Did you pay enough to get any weapons in?"

Despite the situation, Bolan had to laugh. "This end may be fine, but I wouldn't try my chances back in the States. No, I'm light."

The cab driver slipped his hand into the glove compartment and pulled out an old revolver, handing it over the backseat. "Then in that case you take this, my friend. It will allow me to concentrate on my driving."

Bolan took the revolver, an old British Webley service

revolver. Bolan felt the heavy weight in his hands and quickly checked it over. It had been cleaned and oiled recently, and despite its age had been kept in good condition. It was fully loaded.

"Spare ammunition?" Bolan asked. But before the question had even fallen fully from his lips, a box was handed over the backseat.

"My father gave me that," the cab driver said. "He was not in the British army, but he knew how to fight. He taught me. Do not waste the ammunition. It is bloody expensive, and I will charge you," the cab driver said with a straight face.

By now the bikers had throttled and were catching the cab as the driver slowly stepped on the gas, keeping a good distance but allowing them to gain ground on him.

"Wait for the whites of their eyes, as they say in your old films," the driver muttered. "And hold tight."

The cab veered around another corner at the far end of the street, doubling back on its direction as it came out into a residential street, wider than the one they had just left, with low-level adobe houses that had front yards with some livestock and scrub grass. The road was quieter, the traffic coming toward them veering from their path as it noted the bikers now in their wake.

Bolan lowered the window on the rear door of the cab and leaned out, steadying his arm on the door frame. The Webley had a hell of a kick, and the erratic swerve of the cab's balding tires on the road did not help him to keep an accurate aim. Regardless, although his first shot flew high, the second hit home. The bikers were fanned out, with the rider on each flank slightly in advance of the two in center. The man on Bolan's right parted company with his bike as the heavy slug hit him in the center of the chest. He didn't so much fly backward as stay still in the air while the bike beneath him moved forward, suddenly riderless and skittering across the rough road. If Bolan had been lucky, then the bike would have careered into one of the other riders. However, the bike skidded harmlessly to a halt at the curb.

The bikers responded by starting to weave, making it even harder to aim with any degree of accuracy. Two of them took out weapons of their own and returned fire. Fortunately for Bolan, they were not the best of shots, particularly when having to move in such an erratic manner. Their shots flew high and wide.

Hitting the cab was not their prime directive. As they provided cover, the biker on the far flank stepped up the pace, gaining on the vehicle. He would soon be at an angle where Bolan wouldn't be able to get a shot off at him.

The cab driver realized this at the same time as the soldier and took his own action. He yelled a warning before stepping hard on the brake and turning the car into a skid that slewed it around, so that as the biker approached at full speed, he found himself staring head-on toward the hood of the cab. It was possible, for the briefest moment, to see the look of horror and resignation on his face as his bike hit the heavy fender of the old taxi with a jarring crunch. The lightweight Kawasaki bike the bandit favored was perfect for speed and maneuverability, but no match for the heavily reinforced fender at the front of a mule of a car. Bolan, who had pulled himself again into the cab as it began to turn, was thrown against the back of the driver's seat with a sickening thud as the bike hit, but that was nothing compared to the flight the biker took over the car, coming to rest with an equally sickening thud on the road. He landed headfirst, breaking his neck.

"Hey, come on, my friend, quick," the cab driver yelled as he recovered from the impact. The two remaining bikes were closing on them, and Bolan did not have time to draw a bead on either. He could see they had hit the brakes as the cab came to a halt but were skidding on the loose surface of the road, fighting to keep control and as unable to open fire as Bolan.

"Door," the soldier yelled, flinging open the rear passenger door so that as it flew out it caught bike and biker full-on.

"My cab!" the driver moaned in anguish, but that did not stop him from doing likewise, his own door catching the biker on his side as he passed, spinning him into the curb and the low brick wall surrounding a yard where goats bleated in fright at the impact.

Bolan was out of the cab and checking his man, who was out cold. Two were dead. That only left the man hit by the cab driver who might be able to give them any information. As the soldier hurried over, he saw the driver rooting through the man's pockets. The biker was out cold, and there were sirens in the distance.

The driver had a billfold in his hand, and he looked at Bolan before glancing down the road toward the direction of the sirens.

"The money will pay for the damage, and there may be some information in here. But I suggest we look at it somewhere else, yes?"

Bolan, after a quick look around at the collateral damage on the road, could only agree as both men clambered back into the cab. The driver muttered a prayer as he hit the ignition, the engine firing at the third try. He turned the cab and hit the gas. Neither man spoke until they were clear of danger.

"Now I will take you to your meeting, Captain America. Take this—" he fumbled a cell phone from his pocket "—I have three others. I will call you in two hours and we will talk more of this when I find out who those ragamuffins were. What is your name?"

"Matt Cooper. Why are you helping me?"

"You know why. Sometimes you feel you can trust. I am Victor Ekwense. You will hear from me again, do not worry about that."

5

Inside the ministry building, the air was stifling. Fans droned in a desultory manner, doing little more than stirring the heat. Men in suits and others in military uniforms moved sluggishly across the floor, and the woman behind the desk showed more interest in her cell phone than in Bolan as he presented himself.

Even when he announced himself and showed her the letter of introduction from Benjamin Williams that confirmed the time and date of this appointment, she did little more than sigh before hitting the button on her switchboard and curtly announcing his arrival.

"Well?" Bolan asked after a short pause waiting for her to say something when she put down the receiver and returned to her absorbing cell phone.

"He will see you. Hey, you!" she called, hailing one of the armed guards and just as curtly telling him where to deliver Bolan.

The guard gestured Bolan to follow and led him to the elevator. When they were inside, the doors closed to the reception area, he said, "Ignore her. She is a rude bitch. They have her on the desk to put off people coming in from the street. You are visiting a minister, and so she should mind her manners."

"Maybe you should report her, get her reprimanded,"

Bolan said, mildly amused by the man's attitude. His reply made it harder for the soldier to stifle his humor.

"I cannot do that," the guard replied, eyes wide in shock. "She is my wife, and we need her salary."

Discretion being the better part of anything in such a circumstance, Bolan held his peace as the elevator ascended. He thanked the guard with a nod, not wishing to risk words, when he was deposited in the minister's front office.

Here he could see that he was on a different level. There was an efficient air-conditioning system, and the woman who was the minister's secretary was distant but polite as she took Bolan's letter of introduction.

"The minister was delayed in a meeting and has paperwork to catch up on. I will let him know you are here. I will make you coffee, yes?"

Bolan thanked her and sat back, expecting a long wait as she went into the office. He was pleasantly surprised when she returned almost immediately, a look of shrewd appraisal on her face.

"I will bring your coffee in. The minister will see you now," she said in a tone that expressed her surprise as she showed him in.

The minister was already on his feet and across the room as Bolan heard the door close behind him.

"Please, Mr. Cooper, sit down, sit down."

Bolan took the proffered hand and seated himself, watching the older man before him as he settled into his own chair. He was of medium height, slightly wizened and had a bend to his spine that suggested a long-term problem. Bolan could guess how he got it, having heard about him from Benjamin Williams. The man was in his early seventies, but his weather-beaten face made him look a decade older. His name was Wilson Oruma, a government minister in charge of a department that carried little weight in the current regime's priorities, a department that had been given to him as a gesture for the service he had given to his country and to his fellow man in a long career.

"We will talk of our supposed business until my secretary has been and gone," Oruma said in a deep, throaty voice. "I can trust her as much as anyone, but she likes to gossip, like many women. They can cause more damage than anyone else because of that."

And so, while they waited for the secretary to deliver refreshments, linger and then finally go with a backward look, yet again, of searching appraisal. During this period, Bolan considered what Williams had told him about Oruma. The old man before him had fought during the struggles that followed Nigeria's succession from the old British Empire, and when the Biafran war had broken out, over forty years before, Oruma had been instrumental in trying to broker peace, but in a hands-on fashion. He had fought the enemy and also his own men when they had been committing atrocities. He had personally saved Williams from a death squad that tried to assassinate the young politician, tracking him down to a house on the outskirts of Benin City and killing three of the assassination squad. Since that day, the two men had been allies, looking out for each other's back and knowing each other as men of integrity.

That baptism of fire, and the subsequent decades, was why Williams had described him as the only man he could truly trust. Looking at the old man as he talked of fertilizers and pesticides, with his eyes elsewhere, Bolan could see what he meant.

Finally they were able to get down to business.

"I have seen the report," Oruma said at length. "I would not wish to believe it. I am not a man of religion—it does nothing but divide—but as long as men believe, then we just have to deal with it."

"You understand that I am not here in any official capacity, and so—"

"You are a salesman to me. That is all," Oruma replied with a grin. "I have arranged for a small group of men who will accompany you on your mission. They have been handpicked by one of the few men in the military who has dared to investigate the Brotherhood."

"How much do you know about them?"

"More now that I have heard that poor bastard's report," Oruma said softly. "You have to understand, Mr. Cooper, that if you are not one of them, then their presence is a shadow. Their aims are to overthrow, of course, but given that they have people here and also in the North—"

"Any talk of religion could be a cover."

"Indeed. They may be Christian infiltrating Muslim or the other way around. My own view is that they use both and are as false to the Christians as to the Muslims. They just want power and know how to play men. I have seen it many times."

"So have I," Bolan said heavily. "I think it's best to put all sectarianism to one side and just call them the enemy of democracy. Can I rely on the men you're giving me to feel the same way?"

"You think their religion may sway them when it comes to combat?" Oruma shrugged. "That is interesting. I think it will not. Their allegiance is to the government, which is not, as far as I am aware, friendly to the Brotherhood. There may be some—"

"But if they were a majority, then Nigeria would be openly supportive of the Brotherhood."

"Precisely. I will lend you all the tacit support I can, but you will also deal directly with the solider I have asked to put together your team. He is outside, I think." Oruma buzzed his secretary and inquired if the man was outside. When confirmed, he bade her to send the man in.

The door opened, and Bolan swiveled in his seat to see a sweating giant of a man in an ill-fitting uniform.

"Mr. Cooper, this is General Franklin Oboko."

As HE LEFT the building, Bolan looked back to see Oboko in the lobby, making a call on his cell phone. He was watching the Executioner with interest, and as their gazes met for a moment, Bolan could see the general's eyes cloud over, disguising his thoughts.

Bolan paused for a moment. The general had greeted him without showing any signs of surprise that he had arrived. Did he know about the bikers sent to intercept Bolan? He had apparently spoken freely in discussion with Oruma and Bolan. He regretted sending Yobo, as the man was too inexperienced. It had been an error in judgment that he wished to correct. Was he aware that Yobo had fingered him as a member of the Brotherhood? Or did he just assume that his cover was safe?

Bolan had arranged to meet the general at the barracks on the edge of Lagos the following afternoon, in order to meet his handpicked team and pick up the necessary provisions for his mission.

Would Bolan be able to trust any of the men the general had chosen? He would have to approach them with caution. Again he wondered if Yobo had been correct in fingering the general. Was it just the resentment and paranoia of a man tortured to the edge of endurance?

When they had spoken of the Brotherhood's base being in the northern part of the country, Oboko had been opposed to that, taking the view that the training camp was in the south region where Yobo had been sent and was more likely to house the heart of the Brotherhood.

"Why," he had asked passionately, "would such an organization make its headquarters in an area where those who are their enemies are so thick on the ground?"

Perhaps because of that very reason. The general was either naive or trying to deflect attention. Bolan was not sure what to think of him but would reserve judgment and watch his own back. One thing was for sure: Oruma believed in Oboko, which would make it politic to hold his peace once again.

From his pocket Bolan took the cell phone that the cab driver had given him and looked at his watch. Ninety minutes had elapsed. He slipped it back into his pocket and hailed a cab to take him to the hotel booked for him. He replied to this cab driver only in grunts and checked in with no further incident. He kept alert for any signs of being followed, but for whatever reason, he was not now a target.

The phone rang. Bolan was presently in his hotel room, looking down on the street below.

"Victor," Bolan greeted him as he hit the accept button. "I hope you have something interesting to tell me."

"If I do, my friend, then I hope you will return the favor," the cab driver replied in warm tones. "I think you must be a very important man."

"Why would you say that?"

"Why else would a man who has just arrived in the country invite himself to be attacked by boys who come from Kano?"

"The region or the city?" Bolan queried.

"You know the country better than you want me to think," Ekwense said. "The city. They are Kano Youth FC, a gang of youth who are getting greedy. They used to just want to mug and rob, but now they have been hanging out with the big boys."

"Terrorists?" Bolan asked.

"You may call them that. They call themselves freedom fighters. They are neither. They are just fools who are being used."

"By whom?"

"I think if you want to know that, then we should not be talking like this on a cell phone that can be scanned. I may already have said too much to you. I am on the move, you are not."

"I can be. I'll be walking west from where you last saw me," Bolan replied circumspectly before disconnecting.

As he left the hotel and hailed a cab that took him back toward the ministry building, keeping watch all the while, he wondered if he should trust Victor Ekwense. He knew nothing about the man, only what he had picked up from observation. Yet what the Nigerian had said to him as they had parted company earlier that day had been right. There were times when like recognized like.

Bolan got the cab driver to drop him a block away from the ministry building and walked toward it. Standing opposite the entrance, he divined which direction took him west and started to walk. Before he had gone more than a block, a familiar battered vehicle weaved through traffic and pulled over toward the curb, slowing to a crawl.

"Hey, mister, are you looking for a cab?" Ekwense yelled at him.

"Beats walking," Bolan replied, sliding into the back.

"You been followed?" the cabbie asked in a normal tone as Bolan settled in.

The soldier shook his head. "No, not that I can tell. What about you?"

"Do I look like a man who will let some fool follow me, my friend?" Ekwense replied in a tone of admonishment.

Bolan grinned. "Then we need to get wherever you're going and out of sight," he said. "As soon as possible."

OBOKO WATCHED THE American get into a cab and drive away from the ministry building. He wondered why Cooper had taken out a cell phone and looked at it and his watch before putting it away without use.

"He is gone," he said softly into his own cell phone. "I will come at once." He disconnected and barked at the receptionist, ordering her to get his car around to the front of the building immediately.

She simpered and smiled, calling his driver and delivering the order while her guard husband watched her fawn over the general with a mounting frustration that he would probably discuss with her later.

The American puzzled him. When Oruma had approached him, he had suspected that he was being set up. The old man had a reputation that meant the Brotherhood had never bothered to approach him as they had other senior politicians. In some ways, he was an irrelevance. He would soon be dead or retired, and the current generation on the street did not remember him. He was only of importance to some senior politicians and civil servants who had worked with him and fought with him. Yet such was his reputation that, until they were gone, it was best not to touch him.

The idea that he was to put together a task force for this American to lead in an attack against the Brotherhood could easily be a trap. He had decided that his best option was to recruit five men who were clean, and insert only one of the Brotherhood's soldiers. One should be enough. The others being clean should keep his position in the official structure unblemished, while still appeasing his other paymasters.

But it was all getting too much. Oboko did not believe in the Brotherhood of the Eagle. He did not care what they wanted. He only knew that, to him, it meant power, cash and the chance for as much pussy as he could get. He was a man of simple tastes, in that way. Power over men was useful only for what you could get out of it, not to build empires. Besides, if the Brotherhood was really as strong as was rumored, then it would be politic to have favors owed to him should they take over.

Nonetheless, the constant juggling was getting too much for him. As his car pulled up at the gates of a walled compound, the driver leaning out to identify his passenger to the camera-phone intercom that opened the gates, Oboko felt an ominous rumbling in his immense gut.

Ordering his driver to wait, he left the car once it had rolled up the drive to the low-level white stucco house that sprawled across the unkempt gardens. As he approached the doors, they opened and he walked into the lobby of the building. Women in bikinis and negligees lounged, waiting for clients, looking perfectly in place among the gilt and plush. An older white woman approached him.

"General, you are expected. Would you like to choose for afterward?" she queried with an expansive gesture at her merchandise.

The general shook his head and mopped at his sweating brow. "I do not think I will feel like it afterward," he muttered.

The woman pursed her lips, nodded and led him through the lobby and to a door that was located beneath the faux-marble spiral staircase. She knocked once and left the general in charge of a cold-eyed soldier. Without a word, he led Oboko through to an office at the back of the house, secured from the rest of the building.

The office was decorated much like the rest of the building, though differentiated by the animal skins on the walls, and the banks of CCTV and computer monitors that were anchored by a large teak desk. Behind it sat a tall, thin man with a shaved head and a knife scar that ran down his left cheek. He gestured that the general be seated in the chair before him.

"Franklin, you have a lot to explain to me before I leave," he said with a smile that didn't quite reach his eyes.

6

Victor Ekwense pulled the cab to a halt outside a bar where men eyed Bolan with some suspicion as he got out of the back.

"Victor, man, no tourists. You know that," one of them muttered as Bolan and Ekwense passed him.

"No tourist," the cab driver replied dismissively. "You come in and listen. You might actually learn something, instead of standing around moaning like an old woman." He carried on, leaving the others outside laughing.

Inside the bar was dark and dingy. A plasma-screen TV played a low-budget Nollywood film where a man and a woman were arguing in a local dialect on a set that looked a lot like the hotel room Bolan had just left behind. He couldn't follow all that they said, but it made the few men and women in the bar that were watching laugh out loud. He was actually surprised that they could hear the TV over the sound of music that bubbled from the jukebox.

The rest of the people in the bar were either seated at ramshackle tables or standing against the wall or the bar itself, talking among themselves. Bolan noticed that a number of glances, not all of them friendly, were directed at Ekwense and himself. He was sure that it wasn't the cab driver attracting the hostility.

Ekwense gestured to the barman, whispered a few

words in his ear and led the soldier through a beaded curtain to a room at the back, behind the bar. As he followed the cab driver, the big American noted that their trip to the back room had caused a few of the glances to change from hostile to curious.

A fluorescent light gave the room a garish white glare that contrasted with the dingy bar area. The adobe walls cut out a lot of the noise, only the thump of the insistent bass from the jukebox cutting through. In this relative silence, he was greeted by stares from the eight men in the room. Five of them were clustered around a table on which they played dominoes, money scattered in front of them and between the tiles and beer bottles that covered the surface. The other three men were leaning against the walls and had been watching the play before Bolan's entrance gave them another spectacle.

"Gentlemen," Bolan murmured as he scanned them. At least two of the men standing and two sitting were carrying weapons, either handguns or knives. That much he could see. It was a fair bet that others were also armed. He wasn't.

"Cool, boys," Ekwense said. "This is the guy I was talking about. The one who had the Kano gang up his ass."

"Did you have to bring him here?" one of the seated men said. "That was not a good idea, Victor."

"Maybe it is, my friend," the cab driver said easily. He moved forward and brushed one of the domino players off his chair. "Let my friend here sit down, Kanu. I think he has a lot in common with us, though maybe he don't know it yet, and neither do you."

Kanu, his pride wounded at being treated in such a manner, eyed the solider suspiciously as he took Kanu's seat. "You better have a good reason for being here," he murmured in an aggressive undertone.

"Is breaking the flight of the eagle a good enough reason?" Bolan said easily, noting the change in expressions around the room.

Kanu's eyes narrowed. "If you have a plan, then it's the best reason," he said softly.

OBOKO LEFT THE back office unescorted and mopped at his brow as he made his way out through the lobby without looking at the women, some of whom were now occupied with new customers. The general was unsteady on his feet, his guts griping as terror clawed at him. In no uncertain terms, it had been made clear to him that the American would have to be dealt with, and no trace left behind.

As he left the house with narrowed eyes and an erratic gait, his condition was misread by one of the new customers. "I want the girl who did that to him," he said excitedly. Any other time and it would have made the general laugh. Not now. This was no laughing matter.

Outside he clambered into the back of his waiting car and sat silently for a moment. It was only when his driver coughed discreetly and spoke his name that he snapped out of his torpor and barked at the chauffeur to take him home.

If things went badly, then it might be one of the last times he would see it.

"YOU KNOW, IT may be that this is the time to finally cut out the cancer."

The speaker was one of the men seated at the table across from Bolan. They had listened to his story in silence, the only interruption being the beat that still thumped through the wall, punctuating his words. He had begun with his encounter that morning, then backtracked to the circumstances that had brought him to Nigeria before detailing his meeting with Oruma and the mission he was to undertake.

"You will never get them out. No matter how far you burrow, you will never get to the root of the stink they cause. That rotten shit will always be there," Kanu said, shaking his head sorrowfully.

"No, you are wrong," the man who had initially spoken said softly. "This land is riddled with stupidity and greed, but it is not a place where people want to live in fear. Not anymore. We are not so young that we do not remember the army before our current president. People do not want to go back to that, but they are stirred by the fear of the Muslim, by the fear of the Christian, by the fear of the different. Men run with that. You must stop them. People here are too busy worrying about food and where they can find shelter to bother about much else."

Bolan found it pertinent that much of what he heard was identical to what Williams and Mars-Jones had said back in New York. Strike at the root, and the branches would soon wither.

"So I'm left with a problem, gentlemen," the soldier said, cutting across the pensive silence. "Tomorrow I walk into a room where I might be assigned six men whose sole job is to stop me at any cost. I have no idea if I can trust any of them. I'm going into the forest with them. What do I do?"

"Get the first plane back to America, man," said one of the men around the wall, with a low chuckle.

"That, sadly, is not an option," Bolan replied.

The man who had spoken at length, but had still not identified himself, leaned forward, gesturing with his beer bottle. "You know, my cousin served under Oboko. The man is a greedy fool. He takes bribes—"

"So does everyone, Samuel," Ekwense interjected, finally putting a name to the face for Bolan.

"No, not like Oboko. He is stupid and does not hide what he does. He is only concerned with satisfying his tiny prick and his giant stomach. He does not believe in anything except Oboko. He could easily be bought by the Brotherhood, but he would not believe in them. He would also want to keep it sweet with the military. He would play it safe. Trust none of the men he gives you, but do not assume all will be against you. What you need is someone at your back—"

"Would you do it?" Bolan asked, looking around the room. "I know you men. You're like me, veterans. You've all fought somewhere, sometime, for something you believe in." There was a muttered agreement around the room that he allowed to die down before continuing. "It's a lot to ask, and I can arrange for you to be paid for your time. If anything happens to you, your family will be looked after financially. The question is, would you want to take that risk?"

Ekwense sighed. "My friend, you knew the answer to that the moment I said I would bring you here. Of course, the money will be good. It oils the wheels and lets us feed our families, whether we come back or not. Let me put it this way. We do not like what we have ruling us, but we know there would be much worse if they should fall."

"And the Kano boys?" Bolan asked.

"Are you sure Oboko did not send them?"

Bolan shook his head. "I can't tell. He didn't act like he was surprised I was there, and from the sound of it, he's not that great an actor—"

"He would have given himself away. That's his problem," Samuel said with a sage nod. "He is their weak link, and maybe you should work on him while you can. Once you are in the forest, then we can follow and cover, but who knows if the man or men he chooses will have his weakness."

"That's something I won't be counting on. I've got a worry closer to home, though. If it wasn't Oboko who sent the Kano boys after me, then that means others know I'm here. I'm not sure Oboko knows who I am, but still there's a leak somewhere along the line."

"Leave that with me, my friend," Ekwense said with a sly grin. "I know now where the Kano boys were staying. Those who were giving them a bed know of their business. I think I will take one of my friends there and see if I can persuade them to tell me what they know."

Bolan nodded. "That would be good. I'll be at my hotel until tomorrow afternoon, when I go to the barracks. They're not sending a car for me, so I'll need a cab. No one will think anything of your picking me up. Meantime, I can sort out the payment so that it can be picked up."

Ekwense extended his hand. "I like you, Matt Cooper. If we play it like this, then maybe we'll all get what we want."

"I sure hope so," Bolan said wryly. "Because if not, my neck's the first on the chopping block."

FRANKLIN OBOKO SAT in silent darkness in his lounge. His bungalow had a large main room, two bedrooms, a kitchen and a bathroom. It was surrounded by a yard on all four sides, with a low wall that was for decoration more than any kind of security. Oboko had sent his wife to bed early, having thrown the meal she had made him to his chickens and slapped her for daring to protest. She would be waiting for him, expecting him to do his conjugal duty. His behavior for the evening had not been an unusual occurrence and was usually followed by makeup sex. The general knew that she would berate him in the morning for not following his usual pattern, but for now he was content to let her fall asleep while he sat waiting.

It was close to two in the morning, and the general was himself asleep when he was awoken with a start by the sound of a window being carefully opened. His hand went to the SIG Sauer that he kept permanently holstered to his hip, a totem of power, but also a sign of how nervous his double life had made him.

"Cool it, General. It is me," a soft voice whispered in the dark. Oboko was so disoriented that he could not, for a moment, even tell which window the voice came from and turned awkwardly in his chair, swiveling his head to determine the direction.

"You were not seen?" he said in a hoarse whisper. The general always had trouble keeping quiet, and he caught himself before he said any more, not wishing to wake his wife.

"I was not seen. Do you think I am some kind of fool, General? I am a soldier, not like you."

Oboko was outraged and rose from his chair, gesturing with the pistol he had drawn. "Do you dare insult me?" he asked in a raised voice. "I will—"

He was cut short by a hand on his windpipe that choked the words in his throat. He panicked and swung wildly with his gun hand, shocked when his arm was trapped in an iron grip.

"Calm down, General. It does not matter what I say to you, or what I think of you. All that matters is that you have cheated your way up the ladder and are in a position to be of use to the Brotherhood. I do not like you, and I do not believe you have the faith I have in the Brotherhood. But I do know that you are my superior in the military, and I will pay you that lip service when we are not alone. I have a job to do, and your job is to brief me. You will do this now. I am going to let go of your arm and your throat, and you will speak softly, and you will not raise your hand. If you do, you might have an accident in your home. Do you understand me?"

Oboko, finding it hard to breathe, nodded as vigorously as the soldier's grip would allow. He was relieved when the man let him go, and he slid back down into his chair again with a sense of relief as oxygen flooded his lungs. When he spoke, it was in a croaky voice quieted against his will.

"I was testing you, of course, and you have passed. Well done."

"Have it how you like, General, just do not waste my time," the soldier said, sitting opposite him. Dressed in a black T-shirt and black combat pants with black sneakers, he was like a shadow. He leaned forward and listened intently as Oboko briefed him on the American, his mission and the part that the solider was to play in eliminating him.

"He must vanish completely," Oboko insisted. "There must be no trace that can be followed."

The soldier nodded. "What of the others? They are not Brotherhood warriors. How can I divert their attention?"

"You will not have to," Oboko said with a chuckle that made his throat hurt despite himself. "Remember, we are taking him into the heart of the beast. Our masters will make sure that there is much to distract them."

"Very well," the solider said at length. "I will be interested to see this man tomorrow. He has already shown some initiative and will be a worthy opponent."

"Eh? What do you mean?" Oboko demanded.

The solider told him of the events of that morning, adding, "You mean he did not say anything of this to you?"

Oboko shook his head. "He acted completely normally. I would not have been able to hide such an event should it have happened to me."

"That much is true," the soldier said with a tinge of humor that had been lacking from his tone so far. "I wonder if this means—"

"I do not care what it means," Oboko hissed. "What I want to know is why I was not told of this?"

"The Kano boys were sent by our masters when they heard of the American's coming."

"How did they know that? I did not tell them."

"Do you think you are the only man who would know of this?" the soldier snapped back. "His presence was known, but not why he had been sent or how much he knew. That we required from you. Now we must find that cab driver. He has seen too much. Do not worry, General. I will not ask you to do any work. There are already men on the job. You just introduce me to this Matt Cooper when he comes to barracks tomorrow, and I will be as wide-eyed and nervous of my mission as the rest of the group."

Eyeing the soldier speculatively, the general doubted that the man before him had ever been wide-eyed and nervous of anything. *Snake-eyed* and *certain* were the more appropriate words. But he said nothing, just watched as the soldier left in the manner he had arrived.

Oboko sat there for some time before rising and walking slowly to his bedroom, where he undressed and climbed into bed beside his sleeping wife. He looked at her and wondered if he would miss her—more to the point, would she miss him—if something happened.

He realized that he would miss her, and also doubted that she would miss him at all. This was a disturbing thought, but it was something else that caused him to lay, staring at the ceiling, until the sun began to rise and the rooster in his henhouse began to crow.

General Franklin Oboko was a very scared man.

7

Unlike the general, Bolan slept well when Ekwense returned him to his hotel. Both men were sure that they hadn't been followed, and Bolan's simple thread traps on the door were intact. Ekwense had insisted that the soldier take the Webley and some spare ammunition, seeing as he was unarmed, and although Bolan appreciated the gesture, he kept the gun in the bedside nightstand rather than too close. At that age, even though it was a well-maintained weapon, he still didn't trust the heavy and ancient piece.

Bolan had the soldier's habit of sleeping light, almost with one eye open, and woke with the sun, refreshed. He called room service and was greeted by a disgruntled night porter, not yet relieved of duty, who grudgingly took his breakfast order, delivering it with a surly displeasure after the solider had showered and dressed.

Having sent the man on his way with a tip to sweeten his mood, Bolan got to the first business of the day. His own smartphone, which had lain unused since his arrival, was switched on, and he hit Speed dial to connect to Stony Man, America's top covert antiterrorist organization, located in Virginia. Unlike the cell phone that Ekwense had given him, he knew that the security placed on his phone would ensure any calls were routed through a series of cutouts and scrambled, unlike the eggs he had ordered, which looked more curdled, but he still forked them into his mouth as Aaron Kurtzman finally answered.

"You're late, Striker. I hope you haven't been laying waste to half of Lagos. Hal wants discreet."

"Hal always wants discreet. He should come into the field again, see how hard that is when others won't play," Bolan answered wryly. "There was a little trouble." He related the events of the preceding day.

"I'll check any links we have detailed for the bike gangs in each city and any terrorist organizations," Kurtzman promised when Bolan had finished. "I doubt we'll find anything concrete, though. These Brotherhood bastards are so far under the radar, they could be mining."

"I wanted to ask about that, Bear. There was nothing in the briefing that confirmed their religious affiliations. I don't give a damn if they're believers in Christianity or Islam, and they've got men in both camps. I'm going to be in the north, and that's more Muslim than Christian right now. The last thing I'll need is to find they've got a whole lot of allies we weren't banking on."

Kurtzman was silent for a moment. "There's absolutely nothing to tie them to al Qaeda or any of its offshoots. I'd put money on that part of their story being true. I don't reckon the Christian angle, either. It gives them one hell of a foothold in the south, so it's useful. I'd look more at the shit they've stolen from freemasonry. The Brits have a lot to answer for in Africa, but it's not usually this."

"I've never met anyone with a true belief that wants to blow hell out of anyone else," Bolan stated. "The secret society crap is a good tool for buying silence, and I guess it's a good way of keeping the hierarchy's real intent under wraps."

"And it works in military situations. Another legacy

of the Brits, though we're not immune, either," he added bitterly.

Bolan, who had seen enough evidence to agree, said nothing. There were reasons Kurtzman felt this way, and now was not the time to find out why. At the back of his mind, he recalled the Ugandan cult that had inducted children into their ranks, training them on weaponry before they could even walk properly, and laying waste to entire villages and communities who dared to dissent, taking the women to breed future soldiers by rape. Their leader was still at large, the most wanted man in the world according to some. That was how zealots worked when they did emerge. The Brotherhood didn't have that M.O. But first, there was another matter needing attention.

"There's one other thing—an important thing. Victor's friends are covering my back, and I said they would be well paid. They have families. If they don't come back…"

"Where's your nearest stash for this mission?"

"Cameroon. Close, but too far for me to deal with it in the time I've got. I need Hal to take care of this."

"Sure thing. What do I tell him?"

"Tell him the situation and to pony up the cash for these guys. He can send the money to the embassy in care of Victor Ekwense. I'll tell Victor to expect it within twenty-four hours."

"Consider it done, Striker. And be frosty out there."

Bolan checked his watch. An hour until Victor would pick him up.

He wondered how the cab driver was spending his morning.

"AGAINST THE WALL, move!" Ekwense screamed, emphasizing the last word with a swing of his baseball bat that caught one of the young men across the shoulders, pitching him forward. He was too slow in getting up for Ekwense's liking, so the cab driver hurried him along with a vicious kick in the ribs. For good measure, he lashed out at two more of the men, cracking ribs on one and smashing the other across the shoulders, hearing the crunch of a collarbone.

"Now you will talk," Samuel said slowly, his harsh low tones carrying more threat than Ekwense's scream. "There is little time, and I have no patience. You understand me?"

There was a muttered agreement from the five men and two women lined up against the wall. All were in various states of undress, their reactions slowed by a combination of weed and alcohol.

Ekwense, Samuel and Kanu had driven up outside the house of the gang where the Kano boys had been seen. It was the early hours of the morning, but music could be heard from the open windows of the house, and the lowered lights cast shadows that enabled them to estimate the number of people inside.

Leaving Kanu to keep watch, Ekwense and Samuel had moved toward the house and over the wire fence, past the bikes and trash that were scattered across the yard. The houses surrounding were at a distance because of their yards, and were silent and dark. The two men figured that the neighbors knew better than to argue with the gang, and so just put up with the noise.

In which case, they wouldn't mind a little more. Ekwense had taken one open window and Samuel another on the opposite side of the house. They avoided the door on the assumption it was barred, even though those inside had been stupid enough to leave windows open wide. Coming in from each side, they had been greeted by the sight of the women performing sex acts on two of the men while the other three watched, giggling and stoned. They only realized that they had been raided when Ekwense brought his baseball bat down on their boom box, killing the sound.

"You will pay for this," snarled the tallest of the men against the wall. "I will find you and rape your wife while you watch."

"Shut up!" Ekwense yelled, bringing the bat across the small of the man's back. He doubled over at the pain in his kidneys, and as he did so, Ekwense hit him again, across the neck. "You will be lucky if I let you live." He stepped back and addressed the rest of them. "Now you will tell me why the Kano boys were here."

"Who? I do not—" stammered the only man not to have been hit so far. His response ensured that he joined the others, Ekwense hitting him across the back of the knees, making him buckle. Samuel stood aside, watching his friend work with admiration. He had memories of their times fighting the military and had thought Ekwense had gone soft. Wrong. Samuel held a S&W Night Guard 386 model, but was pretty sure he wouldn't have to use it.

"Wrong answer. I know they were here. Who sent them?"

"I don't know," the young man answered as he struggled to get up. "We were told to give them beds by Ehurie—"

"Who is he?" Ekwense barked.

"Fence," one of the women answered in a tremulous tone. "Pimp. My boss. He ask them to do it or he keep taking what they rob."

"You are talkative, little woman. Why?" Samuel asked softly.

"I don't want to die."

"Then answer me," Ekwense snapped. "Where does Ehurie live?"

The woman stammered out an address. Samuel raised

his eyebrows as he heard. It was a rich part of town. There was good money in crime, still.

He exchanged looks with Ekwense, and then said, "You know that this is a powerful man. That is why the Kano boys come when he snap his fingers. That is why this scum does what he says without asking why."

"We will have to ask him why ourselves," Ekwense said quietly. "But he cannot know we are coming."

"No, you said—" the young woman cried as she tried to turn around. Before she had completed a 180-degree turn, Samuel had put one shot into her head.

Stirred out of their torpor of pain and intoxicants, the others started to yell—anger, fear and incoherent screams—as they realized what was happening. The remaining woman launched herself at Samuel, and was mid-air when his second shot took her in the chest. The five men were slowed by their injuries, but the pain was deadened by adrenaline, and it was all Victor could do to step back and swing at them, driving them away, as the first one took the swing full in the jaw, breaking it and blacking him out as he fell.

Samuel stepped forward, a calm coming over him that he had not felt since his days as a guerrilla fighter. He took two of them out in two shots, knocked back another with a third, though he was still crawling, and then had to move to one side as the man with the smashed collarbone lunged awkwardly at him. He brought down the stock of the gun on the man's neck as he fell forward, hearing the bones crack.

The remaining two men were closing on Ekwense, and the first burst of adrenaline had started to fade, leaving them slowed by their own pain, pain that Victor was only too happy to add to, striking at each and bringing them to the floor. He finished one with a crushing blow to the temple, and the other—despite his last desperate effort—with a sweeping blow that cracked his neck.

Samuel cleaned up the remaining pair, stepping behind each in turn and putting one shot in the base of each skull. Even before he had done that, Ekwense was halfway out the window, beckoning him to follow.

Some lights were on in the street now, and Kanu had the engine of Ekwense's cab running. He was in the driver's seat, frantically beckoning them and revving.

"Don't flood it, fool," Ekwense breathed as he and Samuel bundled into the back of the car. In the distance were sirens, and Kanu took off with a jolt, spinning the car so that it accelerated in the opposite direction to the approaching noise. In a nervous voice, he wondered out loud if those houses with lights could give a good description of the car.

"Do not worry too much about that," Samuel assured him. "We have cleaned up their neighborhood. Their eyes may be blinded by that."

"And they may think we will come back if they talk," Ekwense added.

"This Ehurie, he will be after us if he finds out who we are," Samuel said quietly. "I think maybe we should go after him first."

"YOU REALLY THINK that's a good idea?" Bolan asked Ekwense as he sat in the back of the cab, en route to the barracks.

"I think we have no choice." Ekwense shrugged. "I know of this man. His home is a whorehouse that is used by many of the military as well as government officials. I have had to take men there who have reason for not wanting to use their official cars, and I keep my eyes and ears open. My mouth stays shut, until now."

"How soon were you thinking of going?" Bolan asked.

"I think we have no choice in that, either. We cannot risk word getting around. We must do it tonight."

"If Oboko wants me to leave straight away, I'll stall him. I want to come with you."

"You think we cannot handle this?" Ekwense asked, amused.

"I think you probably can, but there's no reason why you should have to. Besides, there may be some information of use to me when I get to the north."

They arrived at the barracks, with Bolan arranging contact via the cell phone for 6:00 p.m. The soldier had told Ekwense about the embassy arrangement, and in turn the solider had full details of everything the cabdriver had learned so far. All that could be put on hold for the next few hours. Now Bolan had to meet his official military team and decide if they were for or against him.

Leaving the cab at the barracks gates, Bolan identified himself and was escorted to the section of compound where Oboko had his office. As he followed his escort, he noted the facilities and the bearing of the men he saw on exercise or drill. They were better disciplined than some African armies he had seen. That could work for or against him, depending on treachery.

When he was shown into Oboko's office, the general was squeezed into the chair behind his desk, sweating more profusely than usual. There was an aroma of cheap rum coming from him as he dismissed the escort in a bad-tempered bark. When he spoke to Bolan, it was in a wheedling tone.

"Mr. Cooper, I am glad you are here—"

"Is there any reason I shouldn't be?" Bolan interjected.

"No," Oboko replied, just a little too sharply. "I will just be glad when we can get this mission underway. Keeping things quiet around here is not that easy, you know."

"So I've gathered," Bolan murmured, ignoring the fleeting glance Oboko shot him.

The general heaved himself out of his chair and led Bolan through a far door and into an anteroom where six soldiers waited for him. They rose sharply to attention as Oboko entered and stayed that way as Oboko introduced them to Matt Cooper from the UN, who would be their commanding officer on this mission. He then called each man to step forward so that they could be named for Bolan's benefit.

At the general's order they sat down, but Bolan remained standing as this enabled him to get a better look at them as Oboko outlined the mission, using an interactive whiteboard to point out route and destination. They watched the general with rapt attention, enabling Bolan to study them without being observed.

Two of the men were around six foot, wiry and about the same age. Emmett Habila was the younger by about a year and still a raw recruit. He sat forward, his receding lower jaw moving in silent concentration as he listened to the general. Jacob Emecheta, on the other hand, was squarer of face and more assured, sitting back and taking in everything through drooping eyelids.

Saro Wiwa was shorter and chunkier, muscle running to fat to judge by his potbelly. He was also the oldest, although even this only made him midtwenties. He nervously picked at the skin on his fingertips as he listened. Scars on those hands, and also on the left-hand side of his face showed he had experience of close knife fighting.

Gift Sosimi and Noah Obinna sat side by side, occasionally nudging each other and exchanging a solitary word in emphasis of something the general said. They were tall and muscular but still lean. Their camaraderie showed Bolan they had combat experience together.

The final man was Allister Ayinde. He sat on the end, silent and stony. He was just under six feet and had the demeanor of a man who would rather be somewhere else. Occasionally he would shoot a searching look at Bolan, as if trying to divine why they were to act under orders from this white stranger. He would be the obvious pick as a traitor, if not for the fact that he could not be as stupid as to be so open. Maybe he was the only one Bolan could discount?

It was impossible to tell from this first acquaintance, just as ridiculous as to try to guess. As the briefing ended, and the team decamped to the armory to get their provisions for their mission, Bolan figured that he would have to play it by ear and hope that operations in the field would bring out their true colors.

When they were equipped, Oboko informed them that their flight would leave at 0800 the following morning. A troop transport would drop them in the Yobe region. Tonight, they would billet at the barracks.

"Not me," Bolan interjected. The team looked at him with a mixture of interest and bemusement, while Oboko seemed thrown.

"I had assumed that you would wish to be—"

"Don't assume, General. I have some business to attend to this evening. It's nonmilitary."

A grin spread across the general's face. "Ah, I see… If you need to know of a place—"

The soldier had figured the general, being as he was, would misread his words. Good. Let him think that for now.

"It's okay, General. I've been told of a place," he answered blandly.

8

Ekwense picked Bolan up two blocks from his hotel. It was early evening, and the streets were full of people heading to the bars, shebeens and clubs that littered the main streets of the city, their shacklike appearances belying the cash they could pull in from passing trade.

Having returned to the hotel first by foot followed by a cab that he had hailed on the streets, Bolan had been able to ascertain that he was not being tailed. And despite the crowds on this humid evening, he was pretty sure that he was still alone. He said as much to Ekwense when he settled into the backseat of the cab.

"I have not been followed, either. We're not being picked up now," he added with a glance at his rearview mirror. Given the chaotic traffic at the best of times, Bolan was impressed. It said a lot about Ekwense that he was able to pick out and dismiss any possible tails among the free-flowing traffic.

"I do not understand," the cab driver said, "why they send a team after you and then leave you alone when they fail?"

"I figure they wanted to get me before I made any contact and make it look like a routine mugging. People die every day from gangs like that, right? Except they didn't figure that I'd get lucky and into your cab."

"You flatter me, but I'll accept that," Ekwense said with a grin. "So why no other accidents?"

"Too late for that. I've made contact with the minister, so the only way they can avoid suspicion now is if I die in the field, which is always a possibility."

"They will regret that, I think."

"I hope so," Bolan murmured.

They pulled up at the bar Bolan had visited the night before and passed through into the back room without the attention that the soldier had drawn previously.

There Samuel, Kanu and the three other men from the previous evening were waiting. This time there were no dominoes or bottled beer. A half-empty bottle of rum stood in the center of the table, and each man carried a shot glass, some of which were already empty. Ekwense glanced inquiringly at Samuel.

"One shot each, man. Warm us up, give us courage. No more," the rangy man replied in his menacing undertone.

It crossed Bolan's mind that Samuel could make "Good morning" sound like a death threat, which might not be a bad thing.

Ekwense gave a curt nod and introduced Bolan to the three men whose names he had not caught the previous evening. Buchi, Ken and Achuaba were all heavyset men whose bearings spoke of experience in combat of some sort. Whereas they had been smiling and joking when he had seen them before, now they had serious expressions, and their gazes were flint-hard. Bolan met them with the same stare of intent, receiving nods of recognition in return.

"Glass for me?" he asked, indicating the bottle. Ekwense slipped out to the bar and returned with two. Both men poured a shot and drank some of the fiery liquid, which slipped down their throats like molten lava.

"You know what we are doing tonight?" Ekwense asked them, looking around the room. Their determination made Bolan feel on safer ground. "Okay, boys, then it's time to put the old gang back in action," he said with a wry grin and a mock British accent.

"Our commanding officer was trained by the British and never lets us forget it," Samuel said softly to Bolan. "He was a bastard, but he taught us well."

As he spoke, Ekwense pulled a tattered map of the area from his pocket and spread it on the table. He stabbed at a point that came between two creases on the paper.

"This is where we go. You know why by now. What really matters is how we get in—"

"Have you had the chance to recon and find out what their defenses are?" Bolan asked.

"I know some from when I have been there. There was no way to find the rest today without making them suspicious. We just assume they have everything. What they don't have is a bonus."

Bolan shrugged. It was far from ideal, but he could appreciate the circumstances. "Figures," he said. "The real question, then, is what do we have?"

Ekwense smiled. "Ah, my friend, this is where it pays to have a past, unlike most of the time in this country."

THREE HOURS LATER two cars pulled up half a block away from the brothel. Ekwense, Bolan and Kanu were in the cab, while Samuel drove an old sedan that appeared to be held together by rust, but which had a finely tuned engine resting beneath the hood. This subterfuge had served Samuel well in the past, and he was hoping that would hold true this night. With him were Ken, Achuaba and Buchi.

Both parties got out of their vehicles and scanned the streets. There were a few lights in some of the houses, but in this neighborhood, they stood some way back from the road, with walls rather than the wire fences of poorer neighborhoods. The chances of anything being seen, unless the residents walked down their drives and onto the street, were negligible.

Samuel and Ekwense opened the trunks of their cars and revealed an armory of smoke and fragmentation grenades, primitive gas masks and a clutch of Glocks and mini Uzis with spare magazines.

Bolan picked up a gas mask. "Does this thing actually work?"

Ekwense grinned. "There's only one way to find out, my friend."

Bolan shrugged and took a mini Uzi and Glock, along with spare magazines for each. He was wearing combat pants, and used the pockets to store some grenades while slinging a gas mask around his neck. As he did so, the others took their own share of the weapons and ammunition. They were all carrying much the same as each other, and it crossed the soldier's mind that a little variety—a grenade launcher, for instance, or an AK-47—would have given them a little more scope for the type of action they could take. But they had to use what they had, and in truth there was only one way they could take this building.

Synchronizing their watches and switching off their cell phones—the last thing they needed was to be given away by a call, and Ken in particular was called by women every ten minutes—they split into three groups.

The front of the house was to be left alone. The main entrance gates and drive were lined with CCTV, and the entrance's linked-in phone system made it a focal point for security. Ekwense had seen the strength of the gates and to effect an entry here would be pointless.

Better that they take the rear and the side walls. Kanu

and Samuel took one side, Ken and Achuaba the other. Buchi joined Bolan and Victor Ekwense in scaling the wall at the back of the compound.

The land on which the house and its attendant buildings stood was sparsely covered with shrubbery, and there were no trees lining the walls. That made it stand out from the houses around it. Where they wished privacy, the owner of this house wanted a clear view of any danger, and trusted his reputation to keep prying eyes away.

The walls surrounding were low level, and so it was obvious that any real defenses would lay on the grounds once any intruder was over. Without any tech, it was impossible to tell if there were motion detectors or mines. One thing Ekwense knew for sure was that there was a swimming pool out back of the house, so it was unlikely the area around that would be booby-trapped. It was just the land between, then…

The nature of the building and their lack of intel made anything other than a full-on assault useless. Checking their watches and counting down, the three men at the rear unleashed a volley of grenades that arced over the wall and into the grounds beyond. They were ready for the shock of detonation, but still it was awesome as the men on each side had likewise unleashed some explosive power. The percussion made their ears hurt, even with precautions, and it was with an uneasy balance that they scrambled over the wall and onto the sparse turf beyond.

The detonations had sparked a chain reaction among the land mines that had been planted in a ring around the house, driving them back momentarily toward the walls but also blasting them a path as soon as the shower of earth and rock had ceased.

The three men charged forward as four armed guards came from the back of the house to engage them, carrying MAC-10s that they fired in short bursts. All three men weaved in and out of the craters, making them harder targets. The compound was flooded with light as spots located on the roof of the house began to sweep the area. Buchi fired upward, knocking one out and hearing the cry of a hit guard.

From each side of the house, they could hear similar exchanges as their four compatriots also closed in on the enemy.

Ahead the four guards fanned out, dropping to the tiled area around the pool as they took aim and opened fire again. Ekwense took a pair of them down with two sharp, well-aimed bursts, while Bolan took out the remaining spot that was sweeping over them.

As the compound was suddenly hit by a curtain of darkness, the lights from the house and from the spots still on the side threw the two remaining guards into relief as they fired blindly into the darkness that served to mask the attackers. Bolan took out the guards, but not before a yell to one side of him indicated that the guards had done by luck what they had failed by aim. Turning as the last guard slumped, he saw that Buchi had been hit. Ekwense stood over him, ripping a strip off Buchi's shirt and tying it round the wound in his leg to staunch the flow.

"My shirt, man!" Buchi yelled.

"I'm not going to ruin my own shirt, my friend, and you are not badly hurt if you can complain." Ekwense helped the wounded man to his feet.

"It's okay," Ekwense said to Bolan, catching the soldier's glance.

The two men sprinted ahead, leaving the wounded man to follow at a slower speed, alert to any danger around him. He could look after himself, and they knew time was short.

Inside the building, they moved through the corridors

at the back, pausing only to slam open and secure each room as they passed; there was a confusion of yelling and screaming, interspersed with some sporadic fire. They worked their way through to the ornate lobby, where they came across Achuaba and Ken.

"Clear?" Bolan asked.

Achuaba nodded. "Dead or running. Cowards. They've lost their customers, too," he commented, indicating the open double doors. Receding into the distance, Bolan could hear more than a single car and the metallic clang as one panicked driver refused to wait for the gates to open automatically. Looking out through the doors, Bolan could see scantily clad women running after the vehicles, yelling in anger and fear, some stopping to throw stones at the retreating businessmen, civil servants and ministers who had discarded them in flight.

Half a dozen bodies were scattered around them in the lobby, all but one were uniformed guards. The exception was a woman in a bikini who had a line stitched across her abdomen.

"My fault," Ken said with genuine regret. "She got in the way as she ran. Just a working girl, man… There was no need for her to die."

"It's unfortunate for her. Any of us can be in the wrong place, at the wrong time," Bolan answered. "It's bad luck. We all—" He stopped suddenly, spinning and aiming the mini Uzi up the marble staircase, finger poised on the trigger as he responded to the scuffling sounds from out of sight of the mezzanine. He relaxed when he heard Samuel call out, and the rangy fighter appeared holding the arm of the white madam, who was less than enthusiastic.

Kanu was behind him. "All clear up here. The customers and the girls ran, and the guards came running to us." He shrugged. "Must have spooked them."

"Good," Samuel grunted. "Now maybe this one will tell us something."

The woman spit at him. "I will tell you nothing, you son of a bitch. When Ehurie gets you, then you will know pain." She struggled out of Samuel's grip and tumbled down the stairs, landing at Bolan's feet.

"Ehurie is a smart man. You think this is all he does? Sell stuff people bring him and run this house?"

"Lady, he's not that smart if he keeps someone with a mouth like yours around," Bolan said. "He'd probably cut it out, if he knew what you'd just said."

"I said nothing."

"You just admitted he was more than a pimp and fence. We know about the Brotherhood of the Eagle. That's why we're here."

She clammed up, but her sullen expression was a giveaway. "I don't know what the hell you're talking about."

"You do. Now I figure we've got half hour tops before the military or the police are over this place like a rash. They'll be in Ehurie's pocket and scared to come first off. That's fine. You can make this easy, or I can make it hard for you." He turned to Samuel and Kanu. "What's up there?"

"Bedrooms, places of business." Samuel spit. "Nothing we want."

"This floor?" he directed at Achuaba.

"Guard room, armory, reception for parties," the man replied with a twisted grin. "Nothing for us."

"Nothing out back, either," Bolan mused. "Not the way we came in." He looked around. "There's a big chunk of this place we haven't seen. How do we get in?" he barked at the woman.

She said nothing, but her eyes flickered to the staircase and something covered by a heavy velvet drape.

"Lady, you're no help to your man." Bolan grinned. He detailed Ken and Achuaba to watch the front and sides of the house, sending Kanu with the limping Buchi to cover the back. He beckoned Samuel and Ekwense to follow, bringing the woman with them.

The door behind the curtain was locked. He could try to blow the lock but guessed the electronic pad was on a reinforced metal door. Bolan put his mini Uzi to the woman's gut.

"Open it," he said softly. "A gut wound leaves you a long, painful time to die."

She looked into his eyes but saw only flint cold staring back at her. Unable to read him, her nerve crumbled, and she punched in the code. Bolan pushed her ahead of them and into the secured rooms of the house. He saw the questioning look Ekwense gave him.

"She's no poker player," Bolan murmured. "I always win."

The back rooms were lit but had the dead-air feel of empty space. As they moved farther back, it was clear that Ehurie had left the premises.

"Where is he?" Bolan asked wearily, figuring he wouldn't get a straight answer.

"He's gone north to his people. When we rise and take over the land, the likes of you will know pain."

Bolan and Ekwense exchanged glances. The Nigerian shook his head sadly. "I do not like to do this, usually, but..." He swiveled and rendered the woman unconscious with one clean hit to the jaw.

"Nice punch," Bolan admired.

"I don't like to hit women, but she was annoying me, and we do not have long. The bastard may have left something. We can hope."

While the woman lay unconscious on the floor, Bolan

and Ekwense methodically took the room apart. Some of the outside CCTV was still operational, and they were able to keep an eye on the drive and the road beyond.

The terminal on the desk had been wiped clean, and although there were ledgers kept in a filing cabinet, these related to Ehurie's more usual criminal activity. They were about out of options when Ekwense shot the lock off a desk drawer and pulled out a sheaf of papers relating to the brothel. From the middle of them, a flash drive fell onto the floor.

He picked it up with a grin. "It's small enough to overlook." He shrugged.

"Might be nothing, might be the jackpot," Bolan said. "We'll look at it when we get back. Time to cut and run."

"What about her?" Victor asked, indicating the woman in the room beyond.

"Better not leave her behind. She might be useful. No one should die unless it's necessary."

Ekwense looked unconvinced, but picked her up and slung her over his shoulder on the way out.

Bolan gathered his men, and they made their way swiftly across the back lawn to the far wall. Kanu helped Buchi struggle over, and Ekwense and Samuel manhandled the woman, carrying her between them back to the vehicles, where Samuel cleared the trunk of his vehicle before dumping her inert body inside and slamming down the lid.

"Stay there and be quiet," he ordered, before turning to the others. "We take two routes back, yes?"

Ekwense agreed.

Samuel sniffed the air. "You smell that? Fear, Matt Cooper. No one has come out to see what had happened. Where are the police? This is a powerful man with powerful friends. If we do not stop him—"

"Then we can't afford to fail," Bolan said simply.

9

When Bolan walked into the barracks the following morning, he knew that the next few days would determine whether he ever saw home again. He knew that General Oboko was part of the Brotherhood, although a capricious and greedy man who was led by his appetites rather than any sense of idealism. He knew that the man Ehurie, if not the commander of the Brotherhood, was high in the ranks and with criminal tentacles that spread across the county, intertwining with the grip the Brotherhood had on the military and civil service. And he knew that he had an unknown enemy and a very dangerous one. Somewhere in the corridors of power there was a link between the secret Brotherhood and the three men who knew of his mission. Oboko was out of the picture. There was no way he could have known the details necessary to send the Kano boys.

Benjamin Williams, Adam Mars-Jones and Wilson Oruma. Somewhere in the communication between those three men there had been a leak. Espionage was not Bolan's forte, but more and more it was becoming a part of his brief. He had much preferred the days of pure hand-to-hand battle. A soldier was sure of his ground. Now he had to watch his back in more ways than one.

It was a task better left to those with experience. After arriving once again at his hotel in the early morning hours,

Bolan had called Stony Man and put his theory to Kurtzman. The cyberwarrior found it feasible but was doubtful of what he could do.

"If it's a leak in communication lines, then maybe we can use tech to trace it, and whoever tapped into it. But if it's people, if it's word of mouth—"

"I know. You're thousands of miles away. I'm on site but don't have the time." He checked his watch and realized how literally true that was. "Just do what you can, Bear."

The soldier was able to snatch some sleep, but even as he awoke refreshed for the coming action, the first thing that came into his mind were the events of the night before.

The woman had been talkative. Too talkative. Ehurie would know how big her mouth was and so would never let her near any really sensitive information. Nonetheless, she perhaps knew more than he realized. By boasting of the power her man held, and the fact that he had gone north to start a revolution, she had given away that the destination Bolan and his team were headed for was correct. Oboko's attempt to bluster about the south and the borders along Cameroon had been just that. It was a training camp, all right, but nothing of great import, and could easily be mopped up once the Brotherhood of the Eagle had lost its head.

The woman also revealed that Ehurie had a list of contacts and comrades within the ministries. In her ranting, she had threatened all of the men in the room with the trouble she could bring down. Hopefully this list would be on the flash drive they had recovered: a backup lost in the hurry to move, perhaps. It was encoded, but again Bolan had Stony Man, and the contents had been electronically transferred stateside.

The biggest problem was what to do with the woman. Killing her was not an option. Not just for the morality, but because she could be of use when—and he was determined on this—he returned from the north. She knew faces, names and could be used to rattle those hiding their allegiances. The men who had carried out the raid with him would be leaving, as well. They would dog the military team's footsteps as closely as possible.

So who would keep her captive until their return? Ekwense had a solution, though Bolan had been surprised when the cab driver had taken him to a cellar dug beneath the bar and secured by a hidden, padlocked trapdoor under a wood-burning stove.

"Matt, we watched lots of old war movies when we were young—another thing the British gave us, whether we wanted them or not. But some of those prison camp movies had some good ideas."

The woman, protesting and spitting all the way, had been bundled into the cellar, the door secured and the stove put back in place.

"There is air down there, right?" Bolan asked.

"There's an air duct, and my man who owns the bar will feed and water her once a day until we get back."

"And if we don't?"

Ekwense shrugged. "I'll be beyond caring, my friend, and so will you."

And so Ekwense had returned Bolan to his hotel. Now, several hours later, the soldier had completed any remaining tasks before mission commencement and had taken the car Oboko had sent for him. The driver was Oboko's regular chauffeur, and he eyed the soldier in the rearview mirror as he drove. Bolan noticed that and smiled to himself. Oboko was not such a fool as to trust Bolan entirely. How much of what had occurred over the past twenty-four hours did the general know? And how much was just his suspicions?

The only way that the solider would find out was by facing down whatever the Brotherhood threw at him when they were in the forests of the Yobe region.

BOLAN WAS SHOWN into the general's office, and from there was taken to the briefing room where the assembled team was seated in the same positions as when the solider had last seen them, as though they had remained there, waiting for him. It was now 07:15.

Oboko ran through a final briefing that was succinct and almost curt. He detailed their departure, arrival and the route that was proscribed as the optimum to where the camp designated Brotherhood Headquarters was situated. His voice was oddly toneless, as though he were reciting from memory and had no real understanding of what he was saying.

Bolan looked along the line of men. His team took it all in without question, but Bolan was wondering if the general's tone was in some way dictated by his knowledge that the route and destination were not necessarily accurate. He was perfunctory, as he knew that the camp would be moved, and the route would be lined by soldiers just waiting for the chance to take out Bolan and his team.

Certainly there was no reason to assume that their target plan was accurate. The region of the camp was known. But as Oboko was in charge of the mission at this end, it would be simple to sabotage their destination from the start, and later blame it on poor intelligence.

Bolan had a much better idea: play it by ear, once he was on the ground, and see how the team reacted. If he was right in assuming that there was at least one double agent among them, then a bit of sabotage might force his hand.

The briefing finished, the team was taken from the barracks to a military airfield on the outskirts of Lagos, not far from the civilian airport. There, a troop transport was waiting for them. They decamped and boarded the plane. Oboko was with them, and he avoided Bolan's eye as the solider went through the motions of thanking him and shaking his hand. He had no great desire to do that, but it was a useful exercise. It would allay any suspicions the general had about Bolan's awareness of what was going down, and it would give the solider one last chance to psych the general and try to read him.

The way in which the general's clammy hand limply grasped his, and the shifting of his gaze away from direct contact, told the solider all he needed to know.

Boarding the plane and strapping himself in, the big American gazed around at the men he would fight alongside. All of them had the blank and bland expression of men going into the unknown. If any of them were a traitor—surely at least one had to be—then they were masking it well.

As the plane rumbled down the runway and took off, Bolan shot a last look at his men. Not all would be coming back. Which one?

He leaned back in his seat; he would find out soon enough. Meantime, he wondered how his other team was faring.

"I TELL YOU, my friend, it will be better for you not to come," Ekwense said in an exasperated, exhausted tone.

"I will see this through. We are in this together, yes?" Buchi grumbled as he hobbled across the street to the car. Ekwense followed him, shaking his head.

"You will get an infection in the forest, and that will kill you and do the Brotherhood's work for them. Who will look after your wife and children then?"

"Ken will do that," Achuaba replied from inside the car. "He is very good with that sort of thing, you know."

"Shut up, you fool," Ken growled. He leaned over so that he could see Buchi through the car window. "Listen, he is right. You would help us best—help yourself, too—if you stay here and keep your ears and eyes open. I am sorry to be harsh, but you are crippled right now, and you may slow us down. I don't want to die because you are slow."

Kanu and Samuel had come from Ekwense's house and across the road to where the battered cab was parked.

"Why not shout and let everyone know our business," Samuel muttered savagely. "We will not need to be having this argument if you are any louder. We won't get out of Lagos, let alone get to Yobe."

"He is right," Ekwense added, doing his best to moderate his tone. "Come on, man, don't be stupid. We don't have the time…"

Buchi looked around them. Although it was still early, the street was far from empty, and already they had attracted some attention from those too eager to listen in on someone else's fight.

'Okay," he said sullenly, "but I would like to be part of this—"

"You already are, man. We would not have transport without you," Samuel said softly, clapping him on the back.

The five men crammed themselves into the battered cab and set off for an airfield on the far side of the city, leaving their wounded companion to watch them go. They made their way through the center of the city, which was already at the start of its workday. The roads were crowded with cars and bikes weaving precariously around one another and those pedestrians who braved the dusty roads. Storefronts were open, and trade was already taking place among those on their way to work and those already working. The noise of the city was building toward its midday crescendo, even though that was over four hours away.

Ekwense drove them in silence, each of the five lost in his own thoughts. They had families that they did not wish to leave behind. At the same time, from the moment that the man Ehurie had become a part of their lives, they had no choice but to continue, that they might protect those families. It would have been easy for them to curse Ekwense, and particularly the American Matt Cooper, for getting them involved. Yet he had only been the catalyst for a fight that had been brewing and festering below the surface of everyday life for some time.

They were still silent when they arrived at the small airfield on the opposite side of Lagos from where the military airfield and the civilian airport were based. This was unlike either of them: a wire fence enclosed the area where a single runway strip was laid down, with four small hangars and one shack that served as a control room. The notion that anyone would file a flight plan here was laughed at, and the radio in the control room was used less for discussion between ground and air than cell phones.

When they parked and left the cab in the shelter of a hangar that had one prop plane inside, with an engineer who paid them no attention as he delved into its workings, they made their way to the shack. They were greeted by an old man with an eye patch and a gut that protruded over his jeans.

"I know you," he said simply. "Buchi's boys. Where is he?"

"Hurt," Samuel replied. "Not badly, but enough. You know what we want?"

The old man hawked a glob of phlegm and nodded slowly. "Sure. Don't know why—" He raised a hand to stop

Ekwense as he was about to speak. "Best if I don't know. I know he can fly, but are any of you useful?"

"I can fly. Military service," Ken stated.

The old man looked him up and down with no little skepticism. "I'll believe you. You bring it back in one piece, I'll believe you."

"Has he paid you?" Samuel asked bluntly.

The old man nodded. "Come with me."

He led them across the airfield toward one of the hangars on the far side, away from where they had left the cab. When they got close, the old man jogged ahead and pulled back the hangar door, revealing an old Huey, its paintwork chipped away to reveal some rust and covered in part by a botched spray job that failed to cover its old registration number.

"Shit, man, we won't get far in this thing," Achuaba exploded. "What are you trying to do to us?"

"Wait, wait…" Ekwense moved forward and took a look at the engine. If it was the work of the same engineer who had ignored them on their arrival, then his attention to details explained everything. The engine was immaculate.

"It looks like shit, sure," the old man said with a chuckle. "But that doesn't mean it moves like shit."

"It could be good disguise," Ekwense agreed. "You use this bird a lot? I mean, is it known?"

"Not how you mean. But we use it a lot for transporting cargo, mostly legal. Those who would be bothered are used to seeing it, which is why Buchi wanted it. He's flown for me a lot," the old man added with a grin that told a story of its own.

"It's big," Samuel said, walking around it. "There's only five of us. Do we need something this size?"

"Used to take fourteen people when I found it," the old man said. "Come and look."

He hauled himself up into the belly of the chopper and beckoned them to follow. Once inside, they saw that the body of the chopper had been hollowed out and refitted so that it could take cargo of any kind. Webbing on the sides allowed for support, and there were only four seats other than the two in the pilots' cockpit. On the floor, secured to the webbing, were fuel drums and unmarked wooden and metal crates.

The old man went over to them, slapping them in turn as he spoke. "You got fuel, enough here to prevent you from having to make regular landings. You just need to find somewhere quiet and do your thing. And these are the weapons that Buchi asked for. We've got AK-47s and ammo, but don't ask me where I got them. We got some pangas and combat knives, and some machetes for the bush or anybody in the way in the bush." He laughed, which mutated into a hacking cough. "We also got some grenades for you. Explosive and smoke, and some Russian nerve gas shit that came from Belize. I don't know what it does, I just took it in part payment. I wouldn't use that unless you had to, if I was you."

"We'll remember that," Samuel muttered. "Now, if everything is ready, we have no time to waste."

The old man nodded and jumped down from the chopper. While Ekwense and Ken settled themselves in the pilot seats, Samuel secured the hatch and joined Kanu and Achuaba in the uncomfortable bucket seats that had replaced the originals.

"Man, I swear I will have a broken back by the time we get to Yobe," Achuaba grumbled.

"Man, if that is all you have to worry about, we will be lucky," Samuel replied.

The old man opened the hangar doors fully to allow Ken to lift off a bit to taxi the chopper into the open. The owner

stood back as it passed him and watched as it struggled fit-
fully to lift into the air. He sucked in his breath as it rose
then dipped, and nodded appreciatively as it steadied and
began to rise in the air, turning to move northward. Ken
had been rusty but had soon picked up his old training.

As the old man grunted and turned back to the shack,
dismissing them from his mind now that they were no longer his responsibility, the men in the chopper felt their guts
heave and not just from the changes in pressure.

They were now airborne and taking Matt Cooper—and
by extension, themselves—to their destinies.

There was no turning back. They were on a collision
course with the Brotherhood of the Eagle.

10

While he sat in the troop transport for the long and uncomfortable flight, Bolan considered what trekking through the Yobe region would actually be like. One thing for sure: it would differ considerably from the kind of action they would have had to undertake if they had attacked the training camp advocated by Oboko.

The land down in the southeast, near the border with Cameroon, was dense rain forest. To hack through that in search of a camp that could be easily hidden beneath the dense canopy of foliage would give an enemy ample opportunity to pick off the opposition at will. Oboko would have liked that: to deflect away from the real target and make it easy to dispose of his—and the Brotherhood's—enemy.

Up in the Yobe region, however, it was a far different matter. The savanna terrain in this area, which took them toward the edge of the Sahara, was completely different. Here the plains were covered in tall grass that could easily obscure a party on the ground but would make it easier to pick out anything from the air. The tall trees were occasionally in clumps but were scattered across the sometimes arid plain. In these areas, it was possible to hide and camouflage activity. Accessing them would be hard, but the truth was that the nature of the topography immediately cut down the potential search areas.

In the south, GPS and cell phone signals were disrupted by the overhanging forest and the nature of the terrain. Up here, the plains were plateaus that rode high, making it easier to get the necessary signals.

Bolan was thinking of keeping contact with Stony Man and also with his shadow team. For the former, it was vital that he keep some kind of communications channel open so that, even if he did not make it back, there was still some way of passing on intel. For the latter, the men in whom he put his trust were only recently known to him, and although that had not given him any issues with how much faith he could put in them, it had also not given him the time to make sure that they were well equipped. Their ordnance was not a concern. He knew them well enough to figure they could lay hands on that.

No, the thing that really concerned him was a line of communication between him and the shadow team. All he had was the cell phone Ekwense had given him. It was serviceable, but not high-tech. Reliant on an ordinary network, he had no option but to hope Nigeria's system was up to speed and that the nature of the landscape would help him with any coverage.

Bolan knew he could trust Ekwense and his friends. That wasn't the issue. What he didn't know was how easy it would be to contact them and keep them within range. Or, indeed, to warn them of any dangers that may be directed their way, should they be discovered.

He returned his thoughts to the team given to him as the plane circled to land on the barren airstrip bisecting a run-down military air base in Yobe State. The men with him were unknown quantities. He could not afford to trust them, yet neither could he show any signs of suspecting treachery. It would be a thin line.

The plane circled and was guided in by a man on the

ground. A few soldiers ran along the strip, clearing and sweeping rock as the troop transport made its last approach. The landing was bumpy and uncomfortable, the hard, dry ground unyielding. There were yells of complaint from his men, and some airsickness, as the motion and rough landing churned guts. Bolan watched them, adept at holding down his own lurching stomach. He'd endured dozens of such landings.

The doors opened, and the heat hit them as soon as they dismounted. Drier than in Lagos, it was intense under the early afternoon sun. Looking around the parched strip and the spare grasses that feebly attempted to sprout on the air-base grounds, Bolan realized that to even fashion any kind of rough strip in an area like this was fighting against all odds.

In those few moments, he got an impression of how physically draining the trek toward their target area would be.

A man whose uniform was immaculately pressed— unlike the others he could see—yet was covered in a layer of dust like everyone else, came up to him, saluting smartly.

"Captain Ernest Shonekan at your service, sir," he said in a clipped British.

"Major Matt Cooper, Captain," Bolan greeted him. "Do we have somewhere my men can get a little downtime before we start off? I think the flight and the landing were a little rough."

Shonekan nodded. "We are small and shamefully ignored by our superiors, but we do have food and some beds we can give you for the night. If you are not under pressures of time, I would suggest rest and a sunrise start to defeat the heat."

"That sounds like a good idea, Captain," he agreed, before directing his men to follow Shonekan's direction.

Having seen his men settled in to the Spartan quarters that the air base supplied, Bolan found himself seated in a shack apart from the rest of the base, drinking rice wine while Shonekan played Vaughan Williams on an MP3 player that looked incongruous among the simple 1970s furnishings of the captain's quarters.

"You are wondering why I have this and speak this way, out here," the captain asked with a wry smile, noting Bolan's questioning gaze. "It may seem a trifle bizarre, but my father was in the service before me, and his training was over forty years ago, in the immediate post-Colonial era. He served under military men who stayed on, and their ways were better than those of the fools who replaced them. I saw this, even as a boy, and I prefer to follow those ways. I would choose to be eccentric than corrupt, though unfortunately this is probably why I am posted here, rather than in a city."

"It's a little out of the way," Bolan stated.

Shonekan laughed. "A very British grasp of understatement for an American, Major. If I may turn the tables and be American blunt with you—why the hell are you here? My orders inform me that you are in search of an Islamic terrorist cell. That, sir, is horseshit."

"You think?" Bolan asked, amused. "What makes you say that?"

The captain shrugged. "There are no terrorists in this region. It is true that we have a larger population of Muslim than Christian in this area, but to suggest that this means they are all arming for insurrection is scaremongering. Boko Haram sticks to Borno State. Yobe is one of the least populated areas of Nigeria. There is a reason for this. It is hard living here. You only have to look at the state of this base to understand that. I am here because I do not fit with the military as it is now. I had no sympathy for the regime of my namesake, though I suspect being confused with him in files may have saved me a few times from my own views."

"Which side of the fence do you come down on?" Bolan queried. "Africa is being swept by a hard-line tide. I know. I was in Syria and Libya in recent times."

"I am not surprised by that," Shonekan said reflectively. "It would be one reason for your presence, but—"

"But you have reasons for thinking otherwise?"

"Major, I am no fool, but I truly believe that many in Lagos are. And those who are not have their own reasons for whatever actions they take. Down there, they view as a potential enemy any who do not speak Yoruba or have at least one sister in the Cameroon. I have been here too long. Those few who do eke out a living among us may not share the religion of the south, and they may speak Hausa, which makes them unintelligible to those arrogant fools who will not learn it, but they are too busy trying to farm this shithouse land to bother with guns."

At length, Bolan said, 'That's a fair summation, Captain. And you are correct. I am not here chasing ghosts. I am chasing a real enemy."

Shonekan looked thoughtful. "I am not privy to the knowledge of my fellow soldiers who live in Lagos and pretend they know about the northern regions. If they are sending you here after the enemy that they only pretend to oppose, then they will be sending you to the wrong place—"

"They're here. Maybe not on the map reference I'm given, but they are here," Bolan interrupted.

"I have heard things, but they are circumspect with all. You are to be thrown to the lions, then?"

"I am. My official sources tell me that the Muslim hard-liners have been infiltrated, and this would enable my enemy to live in peace."

"My enemy, too, Major. And there are no real *hard-liners* as you call them. Not here. It is all smoke and mirrors. I can tell you that much."

Shonekan beckoned Bolan to the table that stood in one corner. There was a tablet on the polished wood, and the captain booted up, clicking on a map of the region from his files.

"You see that we are here," he said, indicating an area in the state. "All this area—" he circled for a distance of roughly six miles "—is clear. What references have you been given?"

Bolan indicated an area within the circle. "I'm told that they are around here. That doesn't tie in with your intel."

"Indeed it does not. That is an area of savanna grass. Only a fool would set up base there. Only a fool would go to the middle of nowhere to be ambushed. And you are no fool."

"I try not to be," Bolan murmured. "Where would you base yourself?"

Shonekan thought for a moment before indicating an area four miles to the southwest of the reference Bolan had been given. "This land is covered by trees. From the air it is impenetrable. From the bush, there are ways in. There are no farms or villages within a ten-kilometer radius. There used to be problems with wildlife, but there have been no reports of any incidents for over six months. I put it down to people becoming smart and staying away. But perhaps the wildlife has been driven back, too?" he added with a questioning glance.

"It's worth investigation. It's close enough to the location I was given for the enemy to intercept, engage and retreat before anyone this far off could be any the wiser or could react in any way."

"I would offer you men, mount a counteroffensive, but if I am honest, I cannot trust those under me. Not in this land, not now. They are Christians. I am, too, but I know myself…"

"It's better that we don't arouse suspicion," Bolan agreed.

Shonekan poured another measure of the rice wine for the soldier and raised his glass. "I salute you, Major. I doubt that you can trust those you are with, but I suspect that you may already know that. Perhaps you have a contingency plan. It would be best if you did not tell me," he added with a wry grin.

Bolan said nothing as he raised his glass; but he thanked his luck for sending him an honest man in exile.

THREE LANDINGS IN scrub areas across the length of the country, three hurried refuelings from the tanks held in the body of the craft, and the Huey reached its destination by the next morning. Ken and Ekwense had taken turns to pilot the chopper, as they crossed low over the plains of Yobe toward the map location Bolan had given them. Ken was at the controls, with Ekwense dozing in the seat beside him. In the main body of the craft, Kanu, Achuaba and Samuel also slept. The lurching descent of the craft as Ken brought it down jolted them awake.

Samuel looked at the empty space in the rear of the craft. Kanu caught him, saying, "You think we get here but cannot return?"

"I wonder," Samuel said softly. "Has the old man cheated us? We have used more than half of the tanks loaded."

"True, but we will carry less weight because of it," the younger man replied. "If I am honest, I am more worried that we will not be alive to worry about the return."

The chopper set down and they unstrapped themselves, stretching stiff and aching muscles. As the sound of the engines and the rotors slowed and died away, Ken and Ekwense made their way back.

"Load up. We have time to make up, if we are to be on schedule," Ekwense said without preamble. "They have hours on us."

"Should we try to camouflage the chopper?" Kanu questioned as he picked out his armament.

"There's no way of hiding this out here," Ken scoffed. "Besides, anyone watching will know we're here. All the more reason to move."

The five-man shadow party dropped down from the belly of the chopper and onto the ground below. All around them in every direction, stretching as far as the eye could see beyond the circle cut by the chopper's descent, was a wall of tall, thick grass that towered at head height or above. In the far distances were some clumps of trees, but they were several miles away.

Ekwense checked his cell phone. There was a message from Cooper, sent an hour before. The brief message detailed a new departure time and a new map reference.

"Shit happens fast," Ekwense muttered. His mind raced as to why these two things had occurred. The reasons were maybe irrelevant. If they had any bearing, then surely Cooper would have found it necessary to explain, if only by a word or two. Still he would have felt easier if he could have explained this to his boys. His feeling was made concrete by the mixed expressions of doubt and suspicion that greeted the new intel.

Samuel looked to the northeast of their landing point, where the new map reference would lead them.

"I hope Cooper is sure of what he's doing," he said softly.

HOURS BEFORE, WHILE darkness engulfed the land, Major Milton Abiola sat behind his desk, the only light in the room the glow from his computer screen as he set up the Skype link to Yobe. The office was otherwise in darkness, as was the rest of the building. But Abiola was not in darkness because he wished to be secretive. He was so confident of his position that he would happily have left every light in the building ablaze. No one of any worth would dare to ask him questions.

Regardless, Abiola liked the dark. It soothed him, enabled him to think. It masked his feelings. His scarred face was not a mirror for that at the best of times, but if he sat in darkness as he spoke, then the man he was contacting would not be able to read him. There was no reason why he should not. They had the same end in mind. But Abiola was a cautious, perhaps even paranoid man. What could not be discovered could not be used against him.

"Good evening," he said gently as the face of a man as lean, impassive and snake-eyed as himself came into focus—the man known to Bolan as Ehurie.

"Major, I have been awaiting your call. I trust all is as planned?"

"Oboko has sent the American and has a man within the accompanying party who will possibly do our work for us."

"Possibly?"

"Oboko is an idiot. He still believes I am his superior, and has no idea of his real commander. I left him to put a man in place, but I am loathe to trust his judgment."

Ehurie agreed. "I would like his judgment to be flawed. It would suit me to meet this man sent by the interfering Americans."

"Even more so when I tell you what has happened to your business," Abiola said, keeping his amusement out of his voice. As he detailed what had occurred, it entertained him more and more to see the thunder clouding Ehurie's face.

"What about Anita? What has happened to her?"

"She has vanished. Presumably the American knows where she is. Perhaps you can ask him."

Ehurie gestured dismissively. "She knows nothing of importance. It is my pride they have hurt, not my purpose. I will find out from the American who these others were. I cannot trust you to find them."

Abiola's joy turned in a second to anger. "I am not the one who was so careless as to let one man and some local boys raid my business and kill my men like they were children. You should look to yourself. You may find that our leader's impressions of you have changed because of this."

"Then I will prove myself by killing this American. The time is coming when our leader will need us to prove ourselves. I can do this. You? You have already let him slip through your fingers."

The Skype link was broken at Ehurie's end, leaving Abiola fuming in the darkness, because he knew that Ehurie was right about one thing. Abiola had to prove himself, and the best way to do that would be to recover the missing woman, make Ehurie look stupid and mop up the damage at this end.

He reached for the phone. Oboko. Even the small pleasure of waking the fat fool at this hour made Abiola feel a little better.

11

"This is not the route that the general gave to us," Ayinde said in a truculent tone when Bolan gathered the team together and issued their new directives. "Why is it changing?"

"It changes because I said so," Bolan replied coldly. "Matters always change when new intel comes in."

Ayinde spit on the dusty soil and cast a disparaging glance back toward the base where Captain Ernest Shonekan could be seen with one of his men.

"You think that fool knows anything out here in the back end of nowhere?"

Bolan stepped forward so that his face was so close to Ayinde's that he could feel the man's breath. "It doesn't matter where it came from, soldier. Your job is to obey orders." His tone was cold, and he looked unswervingly into the man's eyes. Ayinde looked away. "Good. Now let's haul out."

The assault team hiked out of the air base with a cloud of uncertainty hanging over it. There was an atmosphere of distrust within them, now. Why had things changed, and why had one of them questioned it in such a manner? Sosimi and Obinna held back, muttering between themselves, while Saro Wiwa formed a bridge between them and the main group, as though already uncertain of the divide. At the head of the group, Bolan set a fast pace, with Habila and Emecheta keeping to that pace while the still disgruntled Ayinde held off their shoulder.

Under normal circumstances, Bolan would not have been happy at such disunity within a team. At this point, however, it might serve a purpose. Now he would be able to see any differences and divisions develop. It may give him some clue as to who he may, or may not, trust. Right now, he trusted none of them. To keep them at arm's length was a good thing. His shadow team would head out to meet him, and he was sure that men from the Brotherhood of the Eagle would be headed for the location he had previously been given. An ambush was the likely object. Very well, he would play them at their own game.

They were trekking by foot through the long grass, which was as tough and unyielding before them as any forest under the growing heat of the sun. It would have been easier to use one of the trucks kept at the base, which is what anyone would normally have assumed, but this would only signal any change of direction to a waiting ambush. It may be a greater effort by foot, but it was more likely to yield results.

Bolan wondered if the shadow team felt the same way.

"Man, this is hard." Kanu sighed as they hacked a path through the grass.

"Save your breath," Samuel said shortly. "You will need it."

These men had no option but to take the route by foot, and they were already discovering that they had been too long in the city life. Once, many years before, they had all been military men and had trekked through forest and bush like this. The heat, the oppression of the grass as it closed around them like a blanket and the constant vigilance for an enemy either human or animal had been second nature. It would take some time to get back those old ways. They could only hope that they adjusted, before something sneaked up on them and it was too late.

Ekwense, who was taking point, stopped and raised his hand. Behind him, the others came to a halt.

"Listen," he said softly.

There, in the distance, they could hear the sound of a truck. It was a couple of klicks to the west, by the way in which the engine whined, and occasional voices carried across the savanna. As they stood listening, it came to a halt, and they could hear men dismounting.

"So, Cooper was right," Ekwense said quietly to his compatriots. "They will set a trap. But we will set one for them."

With a renewed sense of purpose, they began to move forward again, heading toward the truck. Every two thousand meters Ekwense pulled them up so that the sounds of their own progress abated, and they did not mask other noises in his way. Within twenty minutes, they could see the top of the truck above the grass. It was khaki colored, with an open back and the frame for the tarpaulin standing bare, showing that the flatbed back was empty. They could see that there was a driver, still sitting in the cab.

Knowing that it would not be left unguarded, Ekwense directed Kanu and Samuel to move one way, Ken and Achuaba another, so that they circled in a pincer movement. Ekwense would move ahead in a straight line.

Waiting until they were gone from sight, he began his own movement. He was slower, more cautious now. Every step through the grass before him was as light as possible. The one thing he did not want to do was disturb the savanna, motionless in the still air, and alert any enemy.

The enemy, it seemed, was not so cautious. About three

hundred meters ahead of him, he could see the heads of the grasses waving in an erratic manner. He drew the panga from its sheath on his thigh. This was no time for any weapons that made noise. The grass was moving in a wave that would bring whoever was carving that path within a few meters of him. He stood still, poised, his breath shallow as he tried not to give himself away. It was still impossible to see anyone through the thick grass before him, but a ripple of movement gave away his position.

Ekwense waited until he was just past him, and then took a couple rapid strides forward, slashing a path before him with the panga. He knew from the trajectory that the enemy had their backs toward him. He counted on that to give him the vital fraction of a second necessary.

It was over quickly. The grass parted to reveal a man in his early twenties, dressed in fatigues and carrying an AK-47 with the barrel pointed downward. He was tall and thin, and his body twisted as he pivoted at the waist when the sudden sound made him turn. He was still in the act of bringing up the AK when the first strike of the panga cut into his shoulder, slicing down and slipping out of the flesh, snagging for a moment on the material of his fatigues.

He opened his mouth to scream, in pain or fear or warning, but was prevented by a second swing that sliced across his throat, blood bubbling into his mouth and stifling the sound. In shock, he began to fall. Ekwense stepped forward and drove him down, pinning him to the ground and finishing the kill with one blow before coming up quickly, tugging the AK-47 loose and stepping back into the untrampled grass.

It closed around him and he held his breath for a second, his chest burning from the effort. There was no noise—movement, shouting, anything—to indicate that he had given himself away. Gulping in air now, he steadied himself and moved forward again, intent on finding any signs of other men.

He reached the truck. The driver was half asleep in the cab, lazy and relying on his guards rather than his own senses. It was a fatal mistake. Before he had a chance to react, Ekwense had wrenched open the door and grabbed him, pulling him down and stabbing at him with the point of the panga so that it pierced his throat, stopping him from screaming. He stood on the man's torso and pulled the point out before driving it into his chest. He had to tread down hard to pull it out, as the blade was not designed for such use.

Ekwense was still breathing heavily, standing over the man's body when the others joined him, Samuel and Kanu ahead of Ken and Achuaba. Their expressions and the blood-soaked blades they carried told their own stories.

"It has been a long time since I had to kill a man that way," Samuel said softly. "I had forgotten how hard it can be."

Ekwense nodded, then shook himself. "We have no time to waste. Disable the truck, then we head after these bastards. The sooner we kill them and meet up with Cooper, the happier I will be."

"FRANKLIN, YOU LOOK like a man who hasn't slept," Abiola said with a humorless grin as his secretary ushered the general into his presence.

"You know that I have not," Oboko grumbled.

"Sit," Abiola commanded, and when Oboko had done as bade, continued. "You are a fool, but a useful one. You sent the American off with our agent in his party and the right map references, I take it?"

Oboko nodded. "If that was the only reason you brought me here, I could have told you that over the phone—"

Abiola cut him off. "It's called polite conversation, Franklin. Of course I know that you did it. You would have had more than a late-night phone call if you hadn't. No, I have brought you here because the presence of the American has changed things. Even though we can stop him, and without anything that would spark an international incident, he will be followed by others. That is inevitable."

"That is not my problem," Oboko grumbled. "I do what I am asked, and—"

"And you are paid well for it, you fat fool. Now be silent and listen."

Oboko's eyes grew wide, and his jowls wobbled as he bit back on the anger. No one—at least, no one beneath him—spoke to him in that manner. But even though he had an explosive anger, his fear of Abiola was greater. The major knew that, and it amused him to see the fat man contain himself.

"The Brotherhood has worked long and hard to get into a position where we could effect a simple change in power. We have men—like yourself, and like myself—in positions of power within the military. This is also true of the civil service and of many public institutions, as well as the government. There are men in positions of power who are of the Brotherhood and await only the word to make themselves known. One of them is our head."

Oboko looked confused. "But I thought our leader was in the north, and that was why—"

"That is what he wants people to think," Abiola interrupted. "That is what the Americans think because of such misdirection. That is why we will be able to launch our revolution while their puppet is being hacked to pieces by our men." The thought made Abiola smile, for the first time with some humor.

"But why are you telling me this?"

"Because today we start operations, Franklin, and as stupid as you are, you have played your part well. There is still more for you to do before this is over, but before that, our leader wishes to meet you and congratulate you. Come."

Abiola rose and beckoned Oboko to follow. The general heaved himself out of his chair and followed Abiola out of his office and through the building. Oboko was full of himself, puffed out and expansive.

"Of course, Milton, I have always been loyal and you know you can rely on me to carry out any tasks with an efficiency—"

"Save it for your minions," Abiola snapped as they reached a door. "Now be quiet."

The major opened the door. A man was standing, waiting, in the middle of the room. Oboko's flapping jaw dropped and he was rendered dumb with shock.

Abiola ushered him into the room and closed the door behind them. "Franklin, meet your master."

BOLAN'S TEAM WAS only a klick and a half from the map reference that Oboko had given them, but were moving in a different direction, when Bolan halted them.

"Listen," he said softly, and as they stood still and silent in the long grass, they could pick up the distant sounds of movement running almost parallel to them. Bolan grinned; it was as he had suspected.

He had directed his men to split into three pairs and move at angles to the source of the sounds. He kept Habila and Emecheta, and Sosimi and Obinna together, reasoning that the two pairs had an understanding that could be useful. He opted to move with Ayinde and Saro Wiwa, who were not so used to each other.

The men he had with him were newly combat trained, and they moved through the savanna without leaving any traces. Ahead he could see some movement where the Brotherhood men were moving toward the original map reference, and distant to that, other movements that he hoped were the shadow team. But there was no trace of the two pairs he had just dispatched.

Suddenly there were joint flurries of activity in the savanna to his left and to his right, with the sounds of close combat, moving grass and one short tap burst of SMG fire before sudden silence.

Ayinde and Saro Wiwa looked at him questioningly. He shook his head and gestured before them. The movement they had been tracking had momentarily ceased before backtracking on itself. They had been panicked by the attack and were reversing to engage.

Bolan took a path that would intercept them directly and stepped up the pace. Beside him, the two soldiers fanned out so that they moved away from him and were lost in the grass.

If one—or both—were of part of the Brotherhood, then now was a dangerous time.

But there was no time to think about that. His path brought him into line with the men he was tracking. The grass before him cleared, and there were three of them, each with an AK-47. Despite their alerted status, they were still taken by surprise as he burst into them. He was able to take out one gunner with a burst across his chest.

Even as this man fell, one of his fellows raised his AK before Bolan had a chance to turn and fire. He was saved only by the impulsive behavior of the other man, who flung himself forward, attempting to tackle Bolan with a Tekna knife that he had pulled from its sheath. All he succeeded in doing was placing himself directly in the line of fire, so that he took the AK burst intended for Bolan.

His attacker might have been dead but could still cause problems. The AK-47 burst he intercepted had propelled him forward and had increased his momentum so that it was all Bolan could do not to tumble to the ground. If the Brotherhood soldier fired through the man on top of him, there was nothing that Bolan could do.

He braced himself for the impact as he heard another burst. But that was not AK fire, it was from another weapon, and he relaxed as he felt the deadweight removed from him. Saro Wiwa heaved the body to one side, and beyond him Bolan could see Ayinde standing over the dead body of the second Brotherhood soldier.

All his men were equipped with radio headsets but had maintained a radio silence. Bolan now broke it so that they could report in. All four were available and reported mission completed. Habila, however, expressed concern about another party that was still some way off.

"Don't sweat it," Bolan said, watching the moving trail. He gave a rendezvous point, adding, "Don't open fire unless I say." Then, as he moved his two men toward that point, he took out the cell phone and hoped for coverage. Luck was with him, and he texted Ekwense the same coordinates.

Now sure that they had dealt with all of the enemy that were within range, each part of the team made their way rapidly to the rendezvous point.

"Major, these men who are on our tail…" Habila began as they came together.

"Sure—be frosty. They should be with us in a few minutes," Bolan said, calming the soldier.

The seven men waited, all except Bolan, with a sense of trepidation, as they could hear the others approach.

The grass parted, and Ekwense came into view at the head of his team. His eyes widened momentarily as he took in the six men with Bolan, half of whom automatically raised their weapons on sight, despite Bolan's calming gesture.

"Your team did a good job out there, Cooper. I've seen it," Ekwense said hurriedly. "Don't let them practice some more on us."

The soldier allowed himself a grin. "Don't sweat it, Victor. These guys just weren't expecting you." He turned to his team. "Gentlemen, this is my backup, just in case we got caught out. We've already been fed bad intel and set up. Now we're twice as strong. Now we know where we need to head. We're on a tight schedule, but we can do this."

"We've got a Trojan horse, Cooper," Ekwense said with a grin, explaining about the truck. And, seeing Bolan's expression, he added, 'When I was a boy, it was still a British education. Greek mythology not African legends—who would've thought that it would come in useful?"

12

The main headquarters of the Brotherhood of the Eagle was located deep within the forest west of the savanna. For the nerve center of a nationwide organization, it was a surprisingly small compound. Nestled in the heart of the forest and protected from observation by the canopy of trees, any attempts at heat-seeking were thwarted by the area's wildlife and the insulation of the dense woodlands. Infrared devices would pick out a number of confused images, the animals and the tangled woodlands being a suitable screen.

Partly built in trees and partly on the floor of the forest, the base consisted of eight buildings. Barracks and communications huts were up in the trees, supported on platforms that were lashed to reinforced tree trunks. On the floor of the forest were the transport and storage facilities, with both food and water, and ordnance was kept secure on ground level from any predators and also from the elements. There were four trucks not counting the one that had been used earlier in the morning, and in total the base housed thirty-one personnel in addition to the party sent out.

Bolan and his men had no way of knowing all that. They were heading into the unknown and hoping that surprise alone would allow them to gain advantage and gather intel on the run.

Their hope was that in using the truck they had taken in defeating the attack party, they could get into the base before they were discovered.

But that might not be as simple as they had hoped.

"We have one big problem," Bolan said as the two war parties searched the vehicle and gathered the ordnance found there. They had also secured the guns that they had taken off their dead opponents.

"Too many of us," Samuel said softly.

Bolan nodded. "We've got twelve men. There were only six, seven if you include the driver."

"About that," Samuel spoke. He indicated the back of the truck. "We could cover the back, try to disguise it that way."

Bolan shook his head. "Why would they suddenly do that? See that from far off, and it'd just alert them quicker."

"They could be coming back with a greater number if they took some of us prisoner—get their fatigues, dress in them, it could even the numbers."

"That could work. We'd have to hope they weren't looking too closely until we were so close it wouldn't matter, but—"

Ekwense had been listening to them, and interrupted. "Matt, we've got bigger problems than that. We could just run with that. But we can't ignore with the fact that we don't have a destination, and that the Brotherhood will be trying to contact their boys and wondering why they don't answer. They'll be sending men out to follow it up, and we'll be in big shit when that happens."

Bolan grinned. "You know, that's a very good point. We should be worried about that. But maybe we don't have any reason to worry. Maybe we can turn that to our own advantage."

Samuel looked puzzled for a moment, and then a grin of realization spread across his normally grim visage. "Yeah, that's nice. Use their own action against them, maybe knock a few more off their numbers as we go. Cool."

"Is it?" Ekwense asked. "Then for the Lord's sake explain it to me, because you've lost me."

"LOST THEM? How in the name of God can we have lost them?"

"It's a large savanna out there," stammered the soldier standing before Ehurie. They were in a treetop shack, and the soldier kept his hands clasped behind his back, his eyes focused on a spot above his commander's head as he spoke. Before Ehurie had arrived to take charge, they had answered to General Obusanjo, who had headed back to Lagos when his replacement arrived suddenly and without warning. If this alone had not been an indication of a sea of change, then the way in which Ehurie had imposed his discipline since arrival had caused unrest. Three men had been whipped for supposed offenses that amounted to little more than catching the new commander in a foul mood. Anything was likely to make him snap, and the man standing before him now was far too fond of his own skin to want to risk a brutal and random punishment.

Ehurie spit out his reply. "A large savanna? What? You think I expect you to see them with your eyes? With binoculars or a telescope? What sort of an idiot do you take me for? It is no wonder Obusanjo has been called back. Things are too slack here."

The soldier kept his eyes focused on a point somewhere above Ehurie's head. As far as he knew, the two men had swapped positions because something that happened in

Lagos that made it necessary for the commander to get away quickly. This was perhaps not the moment to bring that up.

Instead, he said, "Of course, I was not suggesting that, sir. It is just that we have been unable to raise any of the men by radio, and the GPS on the vehicle has been disabled in some way."

Ehurie gestured dismissively. "It is more likely that your idiot mechanics have not kept it in good repair. Do you not realize what is going on here, man? The American has been sent to flush us out. Those who are against us believe that our leader commands us from here. They underestimate him, of course, but we are still a major communication center. We are like the middle of the spider's web, and all strands come from us. The spider never sits near the center. They cannot stop us, but if we are in some way damaged, then it is like severing the spinal cord, stopping the signals for movement."

"But, sir, I thought that we had a man—"

"We cannot rely on that. We must stop him. I want him alive. I want him to know what pain is. He has allies in Lagos, and I want them." He hit the table in front of him with no little force, making the soldier facing him flinch.

"Find him!" he yelled. "Now!"

Ehurie sat back, his normally expressionless face dark with anger as the soldier left hurriedly, intent on sending out a second party of men. He opened the laptop in front of him and clicked on the Skype icon.

He was not looking forward to calling Lagos, but it had to be done.

BUCHI LEFT HIS house around midday, the pain in his leg deadened by the morphine that Achuaba's medic friend had given him, but still limping heavily. The wound had been checked and was clean, but it would take some time to heal. Right now, time was something that he did not have. What he did have was Ekwense's cell phone number and a need for finding out more information from the woman they had taken from the brothel.

Ekwense had been adamant when they left that all he wanted his friend to do was help the bartender keep the woman secure, fed and watered until they returned. But as far as the frustrated fighter was concerned, she had made a lot of noise and hinted at having information, yet had given them nothing concrete.

She was Ehurie's woman. He would not have let her work in the house like the other women. She would have spent most of her time with him. There had to be a lot that she would know about his activities. It just needed to be pulled out of her.

He would have to be the man to do it. At least this way, he could feel he was being of some use.

It was a short drive to the bar, which was not yet open. Unlike some, this one did not open through the day, its owners preferring to make money through the night.

When Buchi pulled up outside the bar, the bartender was emptying barrels down a drain. He turned to greet the limping man.

"Beer," he said shortly. "Bastard brewer sells me it bad. Good job I haven't paid him yet. No chance I will, now."

"Will he give you trouble?" Buchi asked, partly thinking of the bartender and partly of any attention being focused on the bar at the wrong time.

The bartender pulled up his shirt to reveal a Smith & Wesson .38 shoved into his belt. "Let him try." He grinned. "And you?" he added, indicating Buchi's leg.

The fighter shrugged. "It could be worse. Have you checked on our friend this morning?"

The barman's grin spread. "Let her sleep in a little, I say. There's time enough."

Buchi nodded. "Let me deal with her. I have a few questions I need to ask her, so it will be better."

The barman nodded. "Watch yourself," he said, indicating Buchi's wounded leg.

"Don't insult me, man." Buchi waved him away dismissively and walked into the back area of the bar. He prepared a simple meal for her, and took this with some water to where the trapdoor was hidden. He had an idea of how he would proceed. She would not be inclined to say anything without food or water, and he would give her the chance to answer his questions without any coercion. He hoped that she would see sense, bearing in mind what had happened to her. If she did not, then he would have to use force.

Buchi was a reasonable man. He had been brought up to believe that there were right ways and wrong ways of doing things, like hurting women. The fact that some of the women at the brothel had been caught in the crossfire the night before and killed pained him greatly. He had no desire to add to that.

But this woman was a different proposition. She had knowledge, had colluded in the misery and death of others. She had to be treated as he would treat a man, as he would treat Ehurie if he had him in the cellar rather than the woman.

Perhaps this was why he was stupidly distracted as he moved the stove and opened the trapdoor. He expected the woman to still be dazed from the night before. He did not expect her to be waiting in the dark, almost airless room, poised for this moment.

That the cellar was in darkness worked in her favor. As Buchi pulled open the trapdoor, he could not see clearly into the interior. That allowed her to move quickly out of the dark and at him, clawing wildly. He was taken by surprise and stumbled backward as she cannoned into him. He fell to one side and grabbed wildly, clutching at the woman's dress. The flimsy material ripped without stopping her progress.

Buchi yelled, as much in pain as to alert the bartender outside, while the woman made for the door. He scrambled to his feet, feeling wet warmth trickle down his leg as his wound had reopened, the stiffness now joined by the pain of the newest injury, overriding the painkillers in his system.

As he reached the door, he heard the roar of the Smith & Wesson. The bartender had been in the middle of emptying a barrel, the weight stopping him from leaning forward and grabbing the woman as she passed. Instead, it took him precious time to drop the barrel, which fell at his feet, almost tripping him. His only option was to stop her with a shot, which he snapped off without aim, the bullet flying high and wide.

Already stumbling, and both shocked and frightened by the blast from behind her, the woman pitched forward, tripping over her own feet and sprawling on the ground. Buchi hobbled across the space between them, gaining ground and wincing with every step. The bartender passed him, having climbed over the barrel in his way, and scooped the woman off the ground before she had a chance to regain her feet. She yelled incoherently and tried to pull against him, but he snarled at her and slapped her backhanded across the face, silencing her.

Buchi reached them and pulled at them both. "Quick, get her in before anyone sees," he hissed, tugging them toward the bar and looking around hurriedly.

They manhandled the limp body back into the bar and

tossed her into the gaping maw of the cellar opening. Her body hit the floor with a dull thud.

"What were you thinking, firing like that?" Buchi yelled.

"Me? You fool, why you let her get out like that?" the bartender returned.

"She took me by surprise," Buchi faltered. "I was going to ask her—"

"Man, I don't care about that," the bartender snapped. "Victor asked me to do a job, and you're making it difficult. If this is what you do to help, then don't. You just better hope that no one saw what happened there," he added. "I think we're lucky, and it's too early for anyone around here to be up and watching."

THEY WERE UNLUCKY. Agnes Omanu, who lived three houses down from the converted bar, was up and praying when she heard the commotion and then the shot from the street beyond. Agnes was a God-fearing woman, and the sound of gunfire struck terror into her. But curiosity got the better of her, and she looked out her window, secure in the knowledge that the net curtain and the distance between the yard and the road would be enough to save her from detection. She saw the woman in the road, and the two men lifting her up, one of them hitting her, before dragging her back into the bar.

Agnes picked up her phone and called the police. She had the number on speed dial and was well known at the local station. Mostly they greeted her with politeness to her face and roars of laughter when the receiver was down. Sometimes they came out, sometimes not.

This was not one of those times. Her call was answered by Constable Dele Obey, who treated her with the usual mixture of condescension and disinterest, until she mentioned the white woman. Obey took details and then disconnected the call. But this time, rather than laugh and tell the rest of the station what Agnes had told him, he sat thoughtful for a moment and then picked up the phone again, dialing a number that put him through to a sergeant in central Lagos.

After listening to Obey's story, he told him to wait by the phone and called Major Abiola. In turn, Abiola listened and then called Obey. He made him repeat the story and then commended him.

"You will say nothing of this, but you have done well. It will not be forgotten. I want you to make sure that there are no police patrols in this area for the next two hours, and that any emergency calls from this district can be lost. You will do this."

It was an order rather than a request, and despite the feeling that he had made himself known in important places, Obey still felt a tremor of fear when he put down the phone and implemented the major's orders.

In his office, Abiola sat for a moment in consideration, then made the first of two calls.

"Sir," he said when the phone was answered. "I have good news. Ehurie's woman has been sighted. I have secured the area, and I will be sending men to pick her up. We will soon know what she has told the men who took her. We will know if the American had anything to do with this and if he has allies that we do not know about."

He paused for a moment as he listened to the voice of his leader. In reply, he said, "Of course, sir. I believe you are correct in this assumption. The men who are holding her are undoubtedly allies of those who raided Ehurie's house or perhaps some of the scum themselves. They will tell us soon enough."

He listened for a few moments more as he was told

where to have the captives delivered, then disconnected and made his second call. It was picked up on the first ring, and he was gratified to hear the fear in the voice that greeted him.

"Franklin, it is good to see you in your office so early," he purred. "I have a mission for you."

Oboko mopped at his sweating brow as he listened. As soon as his orders had been delivered, he put the phone down with a mixture of trepidation and relief. He knew in his heart that Abiola was waiting for him to screw up. Despite what the major might say, Oboko knew that his loyalty and competence were a matter of doubt. Perhaps now he could prove himself. He would head this one up himself, and make sure that the woman and the two men told all that they knew.

He picked up his phone and ordered four of his men to meet him with a 4x4 and then checked his own gun. He left his office and walked across the parade ground to where the vehicle was waiting. He gave the destination to the driver and told his men in a few words what their mission was.

As the vehicle weaved its way through the morning traffic, Oboko gulped back the bile of fear that was rising in his maw.

It was time to prove himself.

13

Bolan's men loaded up the truck. It took some time to backtrack and gather all the corpses of the Brotherhood gunners, then strip them down. Their fatigues were cut and ripped in places, and some were soaked in blood. Close-up they would be a giveaway, but from a distance, it might just be possible to fool the enemy as they approached. Bolan and Ekwense sized up those of the military and the shadow party who would fit roughly into the fatigues, and these they then pulled on over their own clothes. The smell was unpleasant but bearable. Those who could not fit into any of the fatigues were to be the "captives," and were glad to be so.

There was a radio in the cab of the truck, and a call went out for the Brotherhood party several times while they prepared the vehicle. The radios on the dead men were either disabled by combat, or were put out of action by the solider and his men as soon as possible.

But all the while, the radio in the cab was a reminder that, with every minute it took them, the suspicion back at base would grow.

"You will have to answer that," Ekwense said to Bolan.

"Leave it until we're ready," Bolan replied. "Give them a broken transmission, let them know it was a hard fight but we're on the way home."

Ekwense grinned. "Make it broken and maybe distorted so they can't hear voices clearly, right?" When Bolan nodded, he added, 'They're speaking Hausa. We need someone who is fluent to answer. If I or Samuel do it, they will hear a Yoruba voice, even though I can speak it."

"Ask the men," Bolan said. "There has to be one of us who can do it, surely?"

"Don't bet on it," Ekwense grimaced. "Bad to fall before the first jump."

While Bolan finished readying the vehicle, Ekwense moved among the men. Eventually he returned with Obinna.

"My mother was Hausa," the muscular solider said softly. "I can speak it like it was my first tongue, even though that is Yoruba."

"I sure as hell hope so," Bolan murmured, casting a look around. They were ready to depart so he directed the Nigerian to answer the calls, informing the Brotherhood base that they were on their way back with prisoners, and it had been a punishing battle.

He listened while the Nigerian made the call. His tone changed as he spoke in the Hausa tongue, softer and more sibilant than the loud, declamatory Yoruba. He had to trust what Obinna was saying, but could see from Ekwense's expression that it was no more than had been asked of him. There was a long, expressive outburst that followed. Bolan had some Yoruba, but no Hausa, and watched the others. When the cheering finished, Ekwense turned to Bolan.

"They congratulated us on a good job," he said with a shake of the head. "Too much praise, man. I don't trust them at all."

Bolan climbed into the cab of the truck. "Better keep it frosty and expect a hostile reception, then. Maybe this will work—"

"But I wouldn't bet on it," Ekwense finished. He looked around at the grim faces of the men in the back of the truck before mounting the cab himself. "I wouldn't lay any money at all."

Bolan would have agreed with him, but at that moment was distracted by his smartphone. Before setting off to engage with the enemy, he wanted to check and see if Kurtzman had turned up any information that would prepare him for the road ahead. What he saw was something altogether larger in consequence.

The trail had been traced, and the possible source of the leak had been identified. If it was correct, then he needed to clean up this end of the mission as soon as possible.

For he now knew that it didn't stop in Yobe; it went all the way back to Lagos.

MILTON ABIOLA HAD a busy morning ahead of him. His duties as a major in the Nigerian army were put to one side, and he left his office to travel the city. While Abuja was the capital of Nigeria, Lagos was still a major center of administration and trade. Secure Lagos, then Abuja, and it would make matters easy for the Brotherhood of the Eagle warriors and loyal brothers in those cities, and other towns and villages, to cast aside the past and come out in their true colors.

So it was imperative that the uprising be timed perfectly. This day would be spent putting men in place, handing them their orders and telling them when to implement them on the following day.

The Brotherhood was a well-oiled machine. It worked on a pyramid system of command so that orders from the leader came down through a small number of lieutenants who then acted by informing cell leaders. In turn, these men would direct those who gave obedience to them. It was ironic that only a very few people knew who the leader was. There was much speculation, and indeed Abiola himself had been asked if he was the head of the organization. It made him laugh. The mind behind the Brotherhood was older, wiser than he was. But if it made those who answered to him more pliable, then such speculation served its purpose.

He visited those who were in civil government and those in the military who commanded regiments. They were instructed to send their men into the field, to be ready for assuming command and overwhelming those who were not of their stripe.

It took Abiola most of the day, but when he returned to his office in the early evening, he found Oboko waiting for him. The general looked disheveled, and was mopping his brow with an even heavier and grubbier handkerchief than he usually carried. When he saw Abiola, he brightened visibly.

"Milton, I have a surprise for you," he said breathlessly.

SEVERAL HOURS EARLIER the 4x4 sped up as it turned off the main drag and headed into the run-down area where the bar was located. The streets were almost deserted, and there was a heavy police presence operating an unofficial cordon, waving the 4x4 through. Those few locals who dared to ask questions were met with a nightstick by way of response, and any who may have followed in their wake took note and kept their peace.

There was an atmosphere in the surrounding area of oppression as word spread by mouth, but not quickly enough to reach the bar, where Buchi was drinking brandy to quell the pain in his leg, while the bartender worked on reinforcing the area around the stove.

"Can't trust that damn woman. Can't trust you, either," he grumbled.

"Man, it's this leg. It distracted me. She wouldn't be able to get past me a second time."

"Yeah, sure…" the bartender muttered as he made his way out back to pick up a loose paving slab he intended to use in anchoring down the trapdoor. He was halfway out when he felt the hairs on the back of neck rise. It was too quiet, and there was nobody around. Even the goats and chickens in the yards had fallen silent. The silence made the screeching tires of the 4x4 as it rounded the corner even more pronounced.

"Quick, out," he yelled, backing in to the bar's back room.

Buchi was not at his best. The liquor and the painkillers had dulled his senses, and through the fog, it took a moment for what the bartender was saying to sink in. By the time he had managed to form a coherent thought, it was too late. The bartender grabbed him and hauled him to his feet, heading into the main area of the bar. Outside, they could hear the 4x4 pull up and the doors slam as the men inside the vehicle poured out. Oboko's harsh voice called out instructions, and all the bartender could think of was dragging Buchi out the front and bundling him into his car before they were caught. Screw the woman. Let them have her if they could find her. She didn't know names, but she did know faces and that would be enough. He should kill her, but there was no time to remove the defenses he had just erected.

Whoever they were—police, military, someone else—they would have to find her and that would take time. They would know him because of his bar, but they would have to find him. He could shelter with Buchi.

If he could get the doped fool out of the building in

time. Buchi's reactions were slow, and he stumbled as the bartender hauled him through the now-deserted bar area.

They had reached the main door when it was flung open and Oboko stood before them, flanked by two of his men. He was holding a Glock, more for effect than intent judging by the angle. That didn't matter, as the men flanking him had their weapons at a business angle. The bartender cursed the fact that he had to support Buchi, as it stopped him reaching for the Smith & Wesson in his waistband.

"Where do you think you're going?" Oboko growled, milking it for all he could. He had a lopsided grin and, after feeling on the run himself for so long, was determined to enjoy the moment.

The bartender tried to turn, reverse his direction, which was not easy when he had the almost deadweight of Buchi leaning on him. It was not worth the effort when he got halfway around and saw two armed men, looking exactly like those flanking Oboko, blocking his path. He cursed to himself and let Buchi fall, fumbling for his gun. He knew that he was a dead man. The only question was would it be quick and clean this way, or would it be slow and torturous as he was questioned here or at military headquarters?

In part, he regretted that, by doing this, he would be leaving Buchi to this fate, but the fool had let the woman free, raised the alarm by doing so and was responsible for the mess they were facing.

Screw Buchi. If the barkeep was going to die, he would take at least one of these cold-hearted bastards with him.

He had the Smith & Wesson out of his waistband and halfway level when the first volley of fire hit him. The two men standing at the rear of the bar both fired a shot, one catching him around the groin, the other in the upper chest. Each impact felt like liquid fire that turned to ice, and each pulled him in a different direction. He squeezed the trigger, but his gun went off in slow motion, the sound of the detonation long-drawn-out and echoing as his vision began to fade. In the distance, as his sight narrowed to a tunnel, he heard glass shattering and knew that he had fired wildly, hitting a bottle behind the bar. He heard the voice of Oboko, roaring like a slowed-down lion, and knew that he had failed to take life for life. The last thing he did before the lights went out was curse his appalling fortune.

"You idiots, you stupid—" Oboko was beyond words. He had wanted the man alive. Not just because he relished the thought of exercising power he rarely felt and making the man talk, but also because time was of the essence. Already he could see that, in this one-story building, the woman he sought was nowhere obvious. He didn't want to waste time looking, partly because there was little available, but mostly because he was useless at things like searches and was in no mood to look like an idiot in front of his men.

He strode across the room, kicking the bartender's corpse as he passed, and hit both his men on the side of the head.

"I wanted him alive. How else are we going to find this woman?" he yelled before turning to those men who were still guarding the front. He pointed at Buchi, who was struggling to pull himself to his feet. "This one," he yelled. "I do not know what is wrong with him, but I want him talking. Now."

They moved forward quickly and dragged the doped man to his feet. One of them reached behind the bar for the hose connected to the soda tanks and squirted him full in the face. The force choked Buchi, and he struggled in their grip.

"Seat him," Oboko commanded, and they sat him on one of the chairs ranged around the bar. Oboko came up to him, bending so that their eyes met. "Who are you, little man? And where is Ehurie's woman?"

Buchi summoned what reserves he had and spit in Oboko's face. The general roared with anger and forgot himself, backhanding his prisoner so that he went sprawling across the floor, landing near the bartender's corpse. That alone was enough to rouse him, and he tried once more to struggle to his feet.

"Take this place apart," Oboko shouted, stepping over and kicking Buchi in the ribs as he tried to rise, knocking the breath from him and careering him sideways into the wood and tin sheeting of the bar.

While the four men began to swiftly and methodically take the front and back room apart, Oboko picked up Buchi with one hand, showing that his flab belied an immense strength. He dangled the man in front of him, slapping him repeatedly as he intoned, "Where is she?"

The soldiers had now finished with the bar and the back room, and had moved on to the kitchen area while Oboko continued his own line of questioning. He was getting nowhere, but rather than get frustrated, he was starting to enjoy the glazed look and the whimpers of pain that he was eliciting from his victim.

It was one of the men in the kitchen who noticed the odd way in which the floor had recently been torn and replaced, and after removing the reinforced sheeting that the barman had spent the earlier part of the morning putting down, he moved the stove and found the trapdoor.

"General, sir, here," he called.

Oboko let Buchi drop to the floor, cuffing him so that he would not stand in a hurry, and gestured one of the men to watch the prisoner while Oboko pushed his way into the back. He got there just as one of his men levered open the trapdoor, and the woman emerged blinking into the light.

She was more cautious this time as she emerged, still injured from being thrown back in, and for a moment she could not believe what she saw. Then, crying, she threw herself into Oboko's arms.

"I never thought I'd be glad to see you," she sobbed.

SHE WAS NOT saying that a few hours later as she sat strapped to a chair in a basement room at the military and civil service building where Oboko had his office. Across from her, Buchi was tied to a similar chair, with his feet in a bowl of water and electrodes attached to his testicles. Oboko was calmly asking him over and over the names of the men he had worked with in taking the woman and ransacking Ehurie's house. Buchi refused to answer, and the current got stronger with each turn of the dial. It was primitive, but these ways still worked best. There was no time for sophistication, only for simple pain.

Occasionally Oboko would turn to her. "You will be next. All that you told them. I need to know."

"I'll tell you all that I knew. I swear I did not tell them, but I will tell you so that you know I am being truthful."

Oboko smiled, though it was more of a leer. "I would not trust you. You are a woman, and you forget I have seen you at work."

She snarled. "You're just going to enjoy this, you bastard."

Oboko chuckled. "Of course I will. But it will also ensure that I get the truth." He returned to his work on Buchi. The electrics were not achieving the full result, so the general took his own personal thumbscrews from his pocket and applied them to the prisoner's hand. Localized pain was less likely to make him pass out; maybe that was just something the general wanted to believe. It had been a long time since he had used these, and he had always enjoyed the reaction they provoked.

But Buchi was strong. His fingers were pulped and bleeding, but still he held out. Oboko found him an interesting opponent, but he was wearying of the task as time was moving on.

It was a knife applied in turn to the soles of the feet and the testicles that finally got the names Oboko wanted. Buchi could not be blamed. Perhaps the painkillers in his system had helped him hold out, but eventually the insane level of pain had made him crack. Ashamed and yet relieved as he babbled and the pain ebbed, he hung his head as he finished.

"Watch and think about this, woman," Oboko said in a matter-of-fact tone. And as she watched in horror, he took Buchi's head in the palm of one hand and drew his Glock with the other. He jammed the barrel into the weeping prisoner's mouth, smiled and gently squeezed the trigger.

The noise was immense in the small room and drowned the hysterical screams of the woman as she could not take in what she saw. She was still screaming when Oboko turned to her. He slapped her face once, perfunctorily, to quiet her, and then said in an even tone, "Now you tell me, and the pain may not end in death. But there will be pain. There has to be."

14

Backtracking over the territory toward the forest was simple. In the long savanna grass the truck that Bolan and his men commandeered left a trail that wasn't difficult to locate and follow. Once they got into the forest, picking up a trail there might prove difficult. If the forest was dense enough, then the men of the Brotherhood would have found it necessary to hack a path in and out, and it would be a matter of locating it and then following back to source. If the forest was not as dense on the ground as aerial photographs and maps had suggested, then they ran the risk of getting lost and being ambushed themselves.

But time was the imperative. All of that went through Bolan's mind as Ekwense directed the truck over the bumpy terrain, hitting the gas as much as he dared on the uncertain ground beneath. The truck bucked and rolled as he wrestled with the wheel. In the back, the men pitched and bumped against one another. The engine whined as it protested against the speed and terrain that it was forced to endure, making it impossible to keep any kind of ear out for other vehicles.

Ekwense was sure that the men of the Brotherhood in the forest knew that something bad had gone down with their men and would be either preparing some sort of welcome or else sending out a secondary party to meet them.

What both Bolan and Ekwense wanted was to get into the forest and out of the open country before that happened. The men of the Brotherhood would have the advantage of knowing the territory in the forest growth; conversely, Bolan would feel on safer ground using his skills and those of his men in such terrain, regardless. There they would not be so open to attack from all angles and would be able to marshal their resources with a greater impact.

In that sense, this was a race against time, more urgent than the other one that Bolan had just discovered.

His reverie was broken by a sudden awareness of the landscape moving in an unnatural fashion ahead of them. It was in an area parallel to the track forged by the outward-bound path of their truck, and it looked like it was moving toward them. The solider tapped Ekwense on the arm and indicated the disturbance. The driver peered in that direction, then a grin spread over his face.

"They know where we are, and they can see us coming. They going to circle us, I think. So stupid that they think we can't see them?"

"I don't know," Bolan murmured. "I figure they're just hoping to outpace and outflank us."

"We'll see about that," Ekwense said with a wink before throwing the truck into a turn that took it off the beaten-down track and into fresh grass, crashing through the thick undergrowth, riding the rough land beneath as he spun the vehicle around and brought it to a halt. In the sudden silence as he killed the engine, complaints and curses filtered through from the men in the back. These died quickly when they picked up the distant drone of another engine.

Bolan and Ekwense were out of the cab before the curses had faded, the soldier beckoning his men to dismount.

"They'll know we've gone off trail and stopped. Fan

out but keep eye contact as much as you can—we can't risk radio contact."

"What do we do with them?" Samuel asked.

"I'd like to take the truck out before they get a chance to send back any messages," Bolan said. "That depends on how far they come before they take the same action as us."

"Then we need to move, not talk," Ayinde spit out. He turned to his fellow military personnel and took it upon himself to detail which of them should pursue which direction. Ekwense looked questioningly at Bolan. He was going to allow this?

"Let him," the soldier murmured. "Put one of your men on each and stay in eye contact. If any of them makes a move to contact but not engage the enemy, then take them out of the game."

Ekwense nodded. "Which one you want to take, Cooper?"

Bolan had been mulling that over. It amounted to which one of them that he trusted the least.

Ayinde. For many reasons, yet all of them could be exactly why he was not the man Bolan suspected him to be. If nothing else, this action would eliminate him from suspicion, although the soldier would have to keep a close watch on his back at the same time. He told Ekwense and the driver nodded, moving off to speak quietly to his men, allocating them each a military man without them knowing of the hidden agenda.

Bolan moved across to Ayinde. "Good move," he said with a nod of satisfaction. "We'll double you as backup if your men take point."

The military man eyed Bolan with a mixture of disdain and suspicion. "You're not going to widen the net?"

Bolan shook his head. "No need, if your team takes a

wide enough arc. The closer they get, the tighter we keep it, the better it is," he said.

With the military man still eyeing him with suspicion, Ayinde directed his men to move. Habila and Emecheta stuck together as always, moving off to the east with Achuaba and Ken on their tails. Saro Wiwa took a more central path, and was shadowed by Ekwense—which, considering the unmilitary girth of both men, struck Bolan as an odd synchronicity. They would be a weak link, crashing through the undergrowth…

Sosimi and Obinna were shadowed by Samuel and Kanu, and they moved out to leave just Bolan and Ayinde standing by the truck. The solider eyed the Nigerian military man. Ayinde said nothing, but gestured for Bolan to follow him as he moved out on the widest western angle of the arc made by his men.

The truck approaching them had slowed uncertainly as the crew had noted that sudden divergence and cessation of their target vehicle. It slewed around so that it was coming across the path already proscribed, and was headed toward the target's location.

The truck's slowing speed made it easy to circle and encompass. It was just fast enough to close the gap between itself and the men on foot, yet not so fast that it reached them before they had a chance to get into position. Better yet, the personnel on the truck were disinclined to get down and pursue their enemy on foot, which kept them all in the one spot.

"Easy," Bolan breathed to himself as the truck bisected the two groups of men, one to the west and the other to the east. Although unable to keep visual observance on the men at the farthest end of the flank, he knew that they were all within sight of at least one other man. From his position, he could see Samuel and Obinna, and the slight movement of grass that signaled the careful progress of Kanu and Sosimi. They were closing in on the slow-moving truck while he followed Ayinde in circling and closing from the rear.

In the open rear of the truck—much like the one they had recently vacated—there were five men, two looking out from each side, leaning over the lip of the flatbed, using the uncovered tarpaulin struts for support. The fifth man cradled an AK-47 across his chest, one foot planted on the flap at the rear of the vehicle, one hand grasping the arch of the tarp strut for balance. He was scanning the horizon, and there was a vaguely puzzled look on his face, as though he was unsure of what he was looking out for.

Bolan could see a grin spread over Ayinde's face as he pulled his own AK-47 off his shoulder and took aim. Bolan wanted to stop him, but it would be hard to do without drawing the enemy's attention to them. His instructions had been explicit—take out the truck before any of the men had a chance to leave it. If Ayinde shot just one man, the alert would be raised, and the fight would be much harder.

There were a few yards between them. Maybe he could stop Ayinde from shooting, but even then, the crashing movement in the savanna that it would cause would still raise an alarm.

If it did, it might still buy them enough time for someone else to throw a grenade into the flatbed. His men had to be in range by now.

Ayinde sighted the unknowing soldier on the rear lip of the truck and began to squeeze the trigger. Almost as if everything was in slow motion, Bolan launched himself across the gap between them. He wanted to stop Ayinde from firing, so his emphasis was on the man's arm rather than deflecting the rifle.

He hit Ayinde side on, barreling him over so that they hit the rock-hard soil beneath the flattened savanna grass, the impact jarring them both. As they hit, Bolan tried to wrestle the AK from the military man's grasp, but it was too late. A report sounded as the rifle discharged uselessly into the long grass.

The man the shot was intended for brought up his own AK in a panic and fired a raking arc into the long grass. His sense of direction was poor, and although the earth and grass near Bolan and Ayinde were raked and pitted by his blast, it was nowhere close enough to being a threat.

The real damage was done by the way that his fellow Brotherhood fighters yelled in panic and surprise, leaping down from the truck. The two men in the cab did not follow quickly enough. They were the unlucky ones, as they were trapped inside when the grenade that arced through the clear, bright sky landed in the flatbed with a dry rattle before exploding, spreading shrapnel that tore through the metal and glass at the rear of the cab.

The blast pitched the men in the back out into the savanna with less control than they would have wished, landing heavily on the bone-hard earth.

Bolan didn't know which of his men had pitched the grenade, but he was glad someone had the wits to do it before the situation got out of hand. He scrambled to his feet, cursing Ayinde. The military man shot him a venomous look but took the matter no further as he, too, scrambled to his feet in order to pitch into the battle that had broken out.

Bolan's men closed on the vehicle, firing into the savanna where the Brotherhood men had fallen after the blast. They had some idea of where their enemies had fallen, but the blast had forced them to look away and take some kind of cover, so they could not be exact. A scream from within the grass showed that at least one man had been hit, but the percentages were poor as the flurry of return fire caused them all to drop to the ground and try to identify where the shots had came from.

Bolan edged through the grass toward where one blast had been visible by a muzzle flash in the grass cover. He kept an eye on Ayinde. The soldier did not follow him, but took off in the opposite direction. Not sure what to make of that, Bolan opted to concentrate on his target. His own gun was pointed down until he got sight of his man. There were too many of his own people in too dense cover to take any risks.

A rustle to Bolan's right drew his attention, and he spun toward it. The muzzle-flash fighter had also been on the move and was running parallel to him. Bad news. He realized that just a fraction of a second after his intended prey. The man rose before him, and Bolan found himself staring down the barrel of an AK from ten yards. He swiveled and brought up his own gun, but knew by the sinking in his gut that he was destined to be just-that-fraction-of-a-second too late. At least he could try and take this guy with him.

The explosion of gunfire made him wince involuntarily as he braced himself for the inevitable impact.

No impact came, surprising him. The gunman facing him dropped his weapon as holes were punched in his back and out his chest. He fell forward and Bolan saw Ayinde standing in the grass, his own weapon leveled and steady.

The military man now faced Bolan head-on, with his weapon at a lethal level while the soldier's was still only partially raised. If Ayinde was the man sent to kill him, then there would never be a more perfect time than right now. Bolan braced himself.

Ayinde, the sneer still on his face, dropped the angle of his gun and beckoned Bolan to follow him.

As odd as it might seem on cold reflection, Bolan's attitude had flipped, and he now felt that he could trust the man. No matter how many of the others may be playing a double game, this man—despite his attitude—was not one of them.

Elsewhere in the savanna, there were exchanges of gunfire as the Brotherhood fighters engaged with the military and shadow teams. This second Brotherhood team was outnumbered three to one now that Ayinde had accounted for one and the grenade for another two in the truck. On one side Sosimi, Obinna, Ken and Achuaba were circling their two men, drawing fire from them in order to pinpoint their position and firing shots into the ground to push them back without risk of stray fire hitting their own men. On the other side, Samuel and Kanu were adopting a less circumspect approach. As Bolan and Ayinde came round to a point where they could see the four men in the waving grass, Kanu and Samuel raised their weapons and hit the two men with an indiscriminate hail of fire that drove them down onto the savanna floor.

Ekwense and Saro Wiwa appeared in their wake.

"You leave us nothing to do, brother," the chubby military man remarked to Samuel.

"Should have been quicker," the laconic fighter replied. By the time the words had left his mouth, he and Kanu were already on their way around to where the other confrontation was approaching an end game. Ekwense followed, in time to see the two Brotherhood fighters surrounded by four of his team—two military, two mercenary—who had their weapons trained on them.

"Drop. Now. Heads down. Hands on head."

Sosimi and Obinna were yelling those words at them, over and over again. The Brotherhood gunners, knowing when discretion was the better part of maybe getting away to fight another day, let go of their weapons, dropped to the dry soil and did as they were told.

"Take their weapons, strip them," Ayinde said as he walked over and prodded them both in the back. "Not so clever now, eh? What unit you come from?"

"We are the Brotherhood of the Eagle," one of them replied in a sullen tone.

"Shut up, fool," Ayinde yelled, reversing his rifle and driving the butt down between the man's shoulder blades so that he yelped in pain. "You know what I mean. Where have you deserted from?"

"I have not deserted," the man replied, gasping between the pulsing of pain as he spoke.

"I don't suppose you have," Ayinde said, sneering. "Your general sent you as part of your orders, I have no doubt. Riddled with scum like you...."

"Give us your location, and we'll allow you to live," Bolan said calmly. "Resist, and we haven't got the time—"

"You do not know the territory there, and you will never find us," the other Brotherhood fighter said. "We may have failed, but they will know that we have failed and that you are coming. We outnumber you."

"We've knocked out two trucks of your men so far," Bolan pointed out. "That's not a bad hit rate. Now are you going to do this the smart way?"

"You cannot make us do anything, and you will surely pay the price for your arrogance."

"Yeah, arrogant...that's us." Bolan shook his head. "So you're not going to do this, then?" He was greeted with silence. "Okay, I guess we'll make you show us the way. Get them up."

He directed Ekwense and Saro Wiwa to lift them up, and indicated they should be taken back to the working truck.

As they marched to where they had left their vehicle, Ayinde dropped back and muttered to Bolan, "You should have disposed of the jackals. You cannot trust them. They will try to lead us astray."

"I realize that," the soldier said calmly. "But I don't kill people for the sake of it. There has to be a reason, and the fact is that I figure these two might just let on more than they know."

"They won't lead us to their camp. You do realize that, right?"

"I'm not that stupid," Bolan said with a grin. "I figure their vehicle tracks should be fresh enough to follow. Besides, I have a feeling that when Ehurie realizes we've taken out a second group of his men, he's going to see red and come charging after us, all guns blazing. He'll count on numbers."

"Exactly. That is why we cannot afford to have passengers. They have strength in numbers."

"Yeah, maybe," Bolan said simply. "But we're smarter. Trust me on this."

15

Ehurie brooded in his aerie, waiting for word from either of the war parties that he had sent after the American and his men. He knew that one of them was a member of the Brotherhood of the Eagle, waiting for the right moment, and he wondered why the fool had not already struck. Even more so, he was wondering why his own men had proved so ineffective.

In number, this was not a large base, but it was important. It purported to be the nerve center of the Brotherhood, and the leader was reputed to sit at the head of his organization from within the center of the forest. Of course, that was not true, but if people thought that—friend or enemy—then it gave the base a cachet and kept the leader from detection in his day-to-day existence. Both of these things were of great importance until the day of rising came. They bound the Brotherhood by faith.

Perhaps its greater importance lay in the fact that it was the centralized communications center of the Brotherhood. The high plains on which the savanna stood gave one of the best areas for coverage and reception from satellite in the whole of the continent. Given the use of electronic media to communicate instantly, this was its greatest asset. Modern communications allowed for a small base that was transportable. Its value in staying put was mostly psychological.

And now all of that was in danger. To avoid scanning of unscrambled communications, the men on the ground at the base still used more traditional radio systems. It was these that gave Ehurie cause for concern as he brooded. Two parties, each of which were equipped, and no word from either. He was certain one had been eliminated, as the communication eventually answered had been suspect. This was why he had sent out the second party. They had appeared to fare no differently.

What power did this American have? With just six men, he had stopped two groups of trained military men.

Ehurie did not know of the shadow team that had joined forces with Bolan. If he had, it would perhaps have increased the deep fear and anger that brewed within him. These were the men who had ransacked his Lagos home and business, and taken his woman.

Things were to drive his depression deeper on that front. He responded to an alert from the Skype on his laptop, and the face of Milton Abiola appeared. Abiola never looked happy, but even by his standards, his face was set grim and harder than before.

"Have you eliminated the American yet?" he asked without preamble.

"I do not know," Ehurie snapped in return.

"What about the men—"

"What about your man?" the base commander rapped back. "Why has he not yet done his job? I should not have to deal with this fool and the military. There are only seven of them in all, and yet—"

"More than that," Abiola interrupted. "We have found your woman. She had much to tell us."

Ehurie's expression darkened as Abiola revealed all that

Oboko had been able to extract from the woman. Ehurie had always been careful to make sure that she thought she knew more than she truly did, and that any important information about the Brotherhood—indeed, about his criminal business that funded his Brotherhood activities— was kept from her. And yet he was appalled to hear that she had been able to piece together more than he would have imagined. She had been more than his trophy and the madam of his brothel. She had used the intelligence she had applied to gather information from customers to gather information about Ehurie. He cursed his own lack of brain for that and cursed again the fact that he kept his brain mostly in his pants.

The fact that the American now had assistance—five other men—accounted for how he had been able to mop up the two smaller groups sent to engage him with ease. Ehurie would be ready for the greater numbers with his next action. More than that, he would look forward to coming face-to-face with the scum who had destroyed his business in Lagos. When the uprising came to fruition, that would not matter to him in any monetary sense. That was not the point. His pride and ego were dented, and assuaging them would give him an extra pleasure.

"Where is she now?" he asked when Abiola had finished.

The ghost of a smile flickered briefly across Abiola's face. Ehurie knew what he was going to say before the words left his mouth.

"Franklin is keen to show his devotion to the cause. So much so that he was a little enthusiastic in his questioning. More than a little, if I am honest. She did not survive long after he had extracted all the information he could. Perhaps that is just as well as she would not have liked the way she looked once she found a mirror again."

Ehurie did not answer. His face was impassive.

"It troubles you?" Abiola queried. "You would like me to deal with Oboko in some way?"

There was something in his tone that suggested he would enjoy this task, but Ehurie chose to ignore it. He waved a dismissive hand.

"I am annoyed that I could not do the job myself and make her pay for the trouble she has caused me. I will just have to take out my anger on the American and the scum he has brought with him," he stated.

He disconnected and sat back, deep in thought. This changed the way he would approach the enemy, without doubt. His initial thoughts of sending out another group of men to meet them were dismissed. That would mean committing a larger party than would be politic.

Let them come to him. He would be the spider. His venom would be lethal.

Ekwense had piloted the truck back onto the path cut by their predecessors, backing up over rough land that made the aging chassis protest and the engine work to its limits. With the other truck little more than a smoking wreck, Bolan wondered if they would have to make the rest of the short journey to the forest on foot. That might have its advantages in terms of avoiding surveillance, but the negatives outweighed them. He had no desire for his men to reach the enemy territory exhausted or at a pace that would allow the Brotherhood to bring their forces into play.

They had to hit as hard and fast as possible, and the truck was vital to that. So Bolan was relieved when Ekwense managed to get it back onto a relatively smooth path and gunned the engine. He hit the trail left by the smoking vehicle in their wake.

"Why this one?" Bolan asked.

"Why not?" The driver shrugged. "They'll be watching both, if they have any sense."

He was right. Whichever of the trails forged by the enemy vehicles that they took, they were sure to be observed. That was why Bolan had no intention of going directly in. The truck was to get them close and quick. Once that had been achieved, he had other plans.

He swung out of the cab and climbed into the flatbed in the rear. Samuel raised an eyebrow.

"You did not think about just getting him to stop?"

"No time for that," Bolan replied. He indicated the two sullen prisoners. "Any words from the wise down there?"

Samuel shook his head. "Nothing. I figure they reckon on us driving right into a trap."

"I bet they do," Bolan said.

"Gentlemen," he continued, addressing himself to all the men in the flatbed, "they have greater numbers, but we have the advantage of being smarter, as the stupidity of their response up to now shows. We also have more men than they're counting on—they only know about the army men I brought with me. So whatever strategy they adopt, we have that edge."

"Are you sure?" Ayinde asked. "You said they would come running, but I don't see them."

Bolan turned and scanned the approaching ridge at the edge of the forest. "No, maybe Ehurie can keep his temper better than I hoped. There's still a lot of forest he's going to have to cover, though."

"He knows it. You do not. Nor do these pigs," one of the prisoners spat out.

"Exactly. That's why I need you."

"You really think we would betray our comrades?" the prisoner asked, incredulous.

Bolan shook his head. "You won't have to. If you don't

tell us, then you get sent in to smoke them out.' He turned to Achuaba and Ken. "You two look about the same size as them. Change clothes and wire them up to grenades underneath. We send them in, and if they get fired on, then the enemy give themselves away and get blown to hell in the bargain."

"You would do that to them?" Ayinde asked, astonished.

"Why not? You wanted me to kill them back there—what's the problem?"

Ayinde grinned. It was the first time Bolan had seen it, and it wasn't a pretty sight. There was also a new respect in his voice that somehow made the soldier feel uneasy as he said, "There is no problem. Smart move, at last."

Bolan left them preparing the two prisoners and swung himself back into the cab of the truck, feeling the wind pluck at his clothes and skin, narrowing his eyes against the dust and grass seed thrown up by the vehicle, riding the bucking of the vehicle as it traversed the earth. All the while, his narrowed eyes were focused on the forest ahead, which grew greater with every second.

He estimated they were about half a klick from the start of the tree cover when he slid back in next to Ekwense.

"Slow her down, but don't stop her," he said.

The driver looked at him quizzically, but shrugged and did as he was asked. As the vehicle slowed to a crawl, Bolan slipped out, keeping pace with the moving ground beneath his feet, and allowed the flatbed section to slip past him. He directed the men in the back to dismount, which they did, pushing the prisoners before them.

Bolan picked up a rock from the ground and moved around so that he was on the driver's side. He beckoned Ekwense to slip out and, seeing the rock in Bolan's hand, the driver realized what he intended. He left the engine running and clutch in, keeping it depressed until the last moment.

As he exited and dropped back, Bolan slipped the rock into place so it jammed on the accelerator. The truck kicked and bucked as the gears whined and it picked up speed. Bolan was spun away from the moving vehicle and landed, rolling, in the long grass. He had been ready for it, and the savanna grass cushioned him as he had hoped.

He rose and dusted himself off, watching the truck weave as it sped toward the path between the trees that led into the forest. He indicated that his men get off the path and into the cover of the long grass before they could be seen, joining them as bursts of rifle and SMG fire erupted from the trees, directed at the truck. The windows shattered, the fender dented and screamed as slugs hit the metal, but still the truck plowed on.

Bolan set off on a circular path that would take his men into the forest by another route, watching all the while as the truck headed on a collision course with the trees.

By the time it hit and exploded, either because of impact or because of the rain of fire, he had already guided his men and their prisoners into the relative safety of the trees.

Now the game was on.

In the cool dark of the forest, out of the harsh glare of the sun, it took Bolan and his men a few seconds to adjust to the change in light. The flora was more tightly packed and dense in this area than where the truck had just crashed, which was why he had chosen to lead them here, figuring that it was less likely to be populated with the enemy. If his guess was correct, the initial thrust of their forces would be directed toward either of the trails into camp, and the appearance of the truck would only reinforce this action.

He gathered his men, with Ayinde listening from a distance, keeping their prisoners both out of earshot and under his baleful gaze.

"We can't use radios in here. It's too risky. We haven't been able to make a sufficient recon of the area, either. For that reason, I don't want us to separate. We spread out, but like on the grassland, we keep visual with the next man."

"This is a big forest," Samuel murmured. "How do we know where we're going?"

"For a start, we follow the tracks made by the trucks. Along the way there, we'll have a lot of Brotherhood fighters to take down. I figure the more there are, the closer we're getting. It's not a subtle approach, but we don't have time for subtle."

Ekwense eyed him curiously. "Cooper, is there something you're not telling us?"

Bolan sighed. "It's not anything I can be sure of, but if you want to see Lagos, Nigeria even, stay as it is—maybe even get better—then we should move on this."

The soldiers were as puzzled as the shadow team, but even though they were not necessarily men of the south, they understood the implication in Bolan's words.

With a somber sense of purpose settling over them, they began to trek through the forest and toward the area where the gunfire and explosion were located. Ayinde drove the prisoners on before him, muttering as he took point, "Stay ahead—too far and I kill you no matter what the American says." The others fanned out in the dense forest, pushing through leaves and branches that overhung and intertwined, forming a thick curtain that made progress slow. The roots beneath their feet caught at their ankles, threatening to tug them down if their attention faltered for a moment. Insects buzzed around them, loud in their ears and biting with sudden pain that only the adrenaline of fear could make them ignore.

The sporadic gunfire at the truck had ceased by now, and the only sound that cut through the hum of the jungle was the crackle of fire as the truck burned, the occasional sharp screech as metal twisted in the heat punctuating the silence.

The relief they had first felt on being out of the direct sun was now replaced by discomfort as the humidity of the enclosed forest started to make them sweat, their fatigues sticking to them.

Bolan had Ekwense to his left, picking his way clumsily through the foliage, and Saro Wiwa to the right. Ayinde was at the far end, with the two prisoners, just ahead of the line. Kanu, Samuel, Sosimi and Obinna came between Ayinde and Saro Wiwa, on the right of the middle three men, while Habila, Emecheta, Ken and Achuaba were strung out between the far end of the line and Ekwense. Bolan could not see each end, but he could hear some of them as they made heavy work of the foliage.

It worried him that their problems in negotiating the forest left them so open. The enemy was in front of them somewhere. The sooner they came on them and engaged, the better he would feel. If you were fighting them, you could see them. Not seeing them was far worse.

Beyond the sound of their own clumsy progress, there were rustlings in the undergrowth that could have been wildlife scuttling to hide but could also have been Brotherhood fighters tracking them. Bolan kept an experienced eye on the bush ahead of them, but there was little that gave anything away.

They were nearing the point where the tracks from the savanna cut into the forest. That was where the enemy had been clustered a few minutes before, and there had been little noise—at least, little audible over their own progress—to indicate that the Brotherhood gunners had moved from their positions.

Bolan held up a hand to indicate that his men should stop—a signal that was passed down the line until all sound dropped, and he could be sure that his men were still.

An eerie silence descended over the forest. Bolan barely dared breathe in case he break that silence.

Then, gradually, as his ears became accustomed to the quieter levels of sound, he could hear in the far distance a wave of rustling, as though moving soldiers had set up a ripple of sound that was spreading toward them, bringing with it danger.

He was not the only one to appreciate its implications. He was about to signal that they move toward the sound when the quiet was broken by the yelling of one of the prisoners. His imploring voice was harsh in the near silence, accompanied by the crashing of foliage as he broke cover and ran toward the ripple.

A cry from his fellow prisoner and an angry yell from Ayinde joined the cacophony. A warning, followed almost immediately by a single shot and a scream, and then…

The forest was suddenly alive with flame and deafening noise as the grenades strapped to the fleeing prisoner's torso were ignited by a single AK shot. Before the vacuum after the blast had even cleared, the air was filled with a blanket of rifle and SMG fire directed toward the blast area.

Directly at the area where Bolan and his men now hit the forest floor, splinters from trees and shredded leaves raining down on them, pinning them to the ground while their enemy stole toward them.

Unless Bolan could act quickly, they were trapped.

16

"Milton, I have done everything you have asked. What more can I do?"

Oboko spread his hands in a gesture of supplication, his eyes wide with fear and pleading.

"Franklin, you have done too much. Far too much. The way you work is messy, and in the transition, we cannot afford messy. It is not good."

"Good?" The general's voice rose from a roar to a screech, fear tightening his vocal cords. "I have gotten you results. Surely that is all that matters?"

Abiola shook his head. "If you really believe that, then you are a bigger fool than I ever suspected. In the coming days, we will need to be seen to be a force for good within the country. We must be whiter than the British ever were," he added with the faintest glimmer of humor.

It went over Oboko's head. "I can be this," he said in a small pleading voice.

Abiola looked around. "I doubt that," he said simply. They were in the basement room where Buchi and the woman had both died. The walls were drab, the once-white paint flecked with brownish-red splashes that may or may not have been blood. The two chairs, straps of leather and twine laying loose, stood mute testimony to recent events, as did the electrical equipment and bowl of tepid water that stood to one side. There was blood on the concrete floor, still red, gathered at the base of both chairs. The major curled his lip in distaste as he looked at them.

"You know I am loyal to the Brotherhood, Milton. I have always believed—"

"Shut up, you moron," Abiola snapped. "You think I do not realize that it is about money and power for you—"

"And you, of course, have no interest in these things," Oboko roared, a flash of anger momentarily overcoming the fear.

"Of course I have an interest in them, but they are not the only things that concern me," Abiola replied calmly. "They are merely the by-products of having a country in the palm of your hand. Of leading a once-great nation back to greatness. In the days before the British, we were a proud continent. We can be again. Our leader has a vision where all Africans realize that they are God's chosen people. We are the cradle of the world, and all wisdom comes from us."

Oboko was, for a second, speechless. He had always known Abiola to be a hard, practical man, so to see the messianic gleam in his eye as he talked gibberish was disconcerting. It may have been best for Oboko to keep quiet at this point, but he could not help himself. If he had any self-awareness, it would have occurred to him that this was always his problem and was exactly what had brought him to this point. But, unaware and undaunted, he continued.

"Are you mad? Africa has always been small areas ruled by small tribes. Great nation? We are something the British put together, like the French made Cameroon and the Belgians the Congo. That is why we have trouble with these borders now that they cut through our old lands. Our strengths were in being small. Even I realize that, and you say I am a moron."

Abiola did not reply. His icy gaze shot through the general, making him shiver in response.

Oboko knew that he had said too much. He had been walking on eggshells for a long time, and when you were as fat in the mouth as in the body, that was not an easy thing to do. He had failed. He had gotten the information that Abiola had required, but he had done it the old-fashioned way. It was the only way he knew.

The Brotherhood of the Eagle was a crock of bird shit as far as he was concerned. Whatever lofty aims they had, it was still about graft and violence. That was the only way to fight your way up. To pretend you were anything else afterward would fool no one. Except, perhaps, yourself? This was what Milton was doing; it was maybe what the leader was doing. Since that revelation, Oboko had been unable to think of the Brotherhood in the same way.

It was all deception—of yourself, of other people—and it would only end in disaster. This was Oboko's sole consolation as he sadly came to terms with his own destiny.

"You are right, Milton," he said mildly. "I do not understand. I think you are the moron, not me. I may be base and coarse to you, but I am honest about these things. I do not dress up what I do in stupid words. I do what I think people want from me, what they ask from me. It is an honest exchange. I do not understand if what you ask is not always what you want."

"You are very talkative all of a sudden, Franklin. Do you think this will save you?" Abiola asked.

Oboko shook his head, a hollow laugh bursting through pursed lips. "Of course it will not. It will not even buy me time."

"You do not want to fight me to save your worthless skin?"

Oboko chuckled. "Why? You have men outside the door. I would have thirty seconds more of life."

"You would have the satisfaction of taking me with you," Abiola said.

"You are not worth it," Oboko said with a sneer.

The general stood motionless, resigned to his fate and just wanting it to end swiftly, as Abiola pulled his pistol from the holster at his waist and leveled it so that the barrel was directed between the general's eyes. Refusing to blink, Oboko met Abiola's gaze as the major started to squeeze the trigger. With his last moments, Oboko thought not of his wife, neither of Abby whose young body he would not taste a second time. Rather, he thought of the American. The general had been scared of him when they had first met, realizing that here was an opponent of greater worth than any he had ever met. If there was anyone who could stop these fools, it would be him.

With his final thoughts, Oboko hoped this would be the case. He finally blinked at the muzzle-flash and deafening explosion within the room.

Blinked, but did not close his eyes again.

The echo died away in the room, leaving a buzzing in Abiola's ears. He calmly reholstered his pistol and looked coldly on the corpse of Franklin Oboko. The general had fallen back as the shot took him cleanly between the eyes, knocking into one of the chairs and pushing it back against a wall that was now stained by his own blood and brain matter, from the larger exit wound. He had soiled himself in death and that along with the cordite and the stench of blood made Abiola feel a little queasy. He nodded to himself and left the room. In passing, he ordered the guard outside to have the room cleaned and the corpse disposed of.

Breathing easier now, Abiola made his way up to his office, where he checked on the progress that had been made during the course of the day. Through the lines of communication, word had filtered back that the Brotherhood of the Eagle had prepared for tomorrow's coup. Those in their departments, regiments and precincts who were not with them would be disarmed and disabled on the following day, giving them the chance to join the revolution or face death. Action would take place in both Lagos and Abuja.

Everything was going to plan. The major left his office and took the elevator up two floors to where the leader of the Brotherhood had his own office. Abiola entered the outer office without knocking and nodded at the secretary as he passed. She looked up, acknowledged him and made no effort to stop him.

He entered the inner office without asking permission. His leader was seated behind his desk, in conversation with a civil servant who had a buff file and a tablet in front of him. They were discussing a problem of budget within the department, and as Abiola entered, his leader looked up with a relief that could only come from an excuse to leave behind complex and dull figures.

"You have news for me?" He noted the look Abiola gave the civil servant and added, "Daniel is one of us, Milton. You may speak in front of him."

Abiola nodded and delivered a concise report while both men listened intently. When he had finished, the civil servant Daniel closed his file and spoke to his superior. "I will go and make ready in my own department, sir. This—" he tapped the file "—is of no importance. It can wait."

When he had departed, the old man behind the desk rose and stretched. For the first time in a long time, his grave expression broke into something approaching a smile.

"They will not dismiss and patronize me anymore, Milton," Wilson Oruma said. "They will pay the price for underestimating me for so long."

UNDERESTIMATING THE ENEMY was something that Ehurie was only too well aware that he had done up to now. He had assumed that the American would be trusting, not that he would arrange backup of his own. That had to be why he had been able to defeat two detachments with such ease. The Brotherhood commander had faith in his men that they would be able to tackle the enemy with ease now that they had the full facts.

With this in mind he had sent men to cover both areas where the forest could be accessed by truck. He was sure that the American would put speed over subterfuge, and that in order to do this he would have to use captured transport, limiting his points of access.

Seated in his treetop office, he brooded on what had happened so far as he sent out his men. He had to keep some back for defense of the base, but he had every intention of hitting hard and fast, taking the enemy down as soon as they hit the trees. Ideally, he would have liked to capture the American and his Lagos boys and make them pay slowly and painfully, but with the coup on the cusp, this was the time to put his own feelings to one side. It was not something that Ehurie had ever done before and was testament to his fear of the leadership of the Brotherhood as much as his loyalty.

His men were in constant contact with him by radio, and he followed their progress eagerly. As the truck approached and was fired on, veering across the track until it plowed into the trees, his heart soared. The fools had played straight into his hands, not thinking he would have time to marshal his sources, and that he would be fooled by their pathetic attempts at deception. Just because a man could speak Hausa fluently did not mean that his voice could not be identified.

Ehurie was full of his own satisfaction when the report

came through that the truck had been empty. That drained the elation from him like the punctured tires on that very truck. He had been trapped by his own hubris. Just as he had thought his mansion impregnable until the American and his Lagos team had marched in, so he had assumed the same of the forest.

He was blinded by his pride, but was not so stupid that he did not realize quickly what the American's tactics were.

"Move out, sector the forest along the line and search. They have set up a decoy, and we have been taken in. I want them dead. Now," he snapped.

Having given the order, the shaved-headed commander ran his hands over his smooth skull and considered whether he should report this to Abiola. Like most men who dealt with the major, he had the uneasy feeling that Abiola looked on him in the same way that he would look at a cockroach and was almost willing him to fail so that he had an excuse to crush him. For that reason, he decided that he should wait until the outcome of this action to make a report. Anything in the interim could only stain his reputation and add unnecessary pressure.

Ehurie left his place behind the desk and quickly descended to the forest floor. All the treetop buildings were empty; all men deployed and in position. Those who were guarding the base itself were either in their secured positions or within the confines of the base floor, where the remaining vehicles and the ordnance were located.

"You, you, here," Ehurie barked, beckoning two men. As they jogged to him on the double, he continued, "Secure the buildings and vehicles. Send word to the outposts. The American and his men are through the outer defenses. We are after them, but there are no guarantees. We are close, and we cannot let things slip now, for the sake of the

Brotherhood. We have a man in their party, but we cannot guarantee that he will be able to stop them."

"How do we identify him so that we do not kill one of our own?" one of the men asked.

Ehurie snorted. "Kill them all. He knows the risks he takes, and he knows that if he is caught in a cross fire, he dies for the greater glory of the Brotherhood."

For a moment, the two men facing him said nothing. Like all those with allegiance to the Brotherhood, they knew that their individual lives were of no importance against the greater good of the organization. But to hear it stated so bluntly, and to know that they had to kill one of their own in the fight to come, was a sobering realization.

"What are you waiting for?" Ehurie growled, dismissing them.

As they turned and jogged back to their tasks, the commander climbed back up to his aerie. Once there he settled back behind his desk, picking up the communications transmitter and snapping out a demand for updates. He listened as each detail returned to him. The burning truck had been left, and the soldiers had started their search. The terrain was thick and dense, with clusters of trees leaving knotted roots that were treacherous underfoot, disguised as they were by moss and grass. Their progress was of necessity slow.

Ehurie was frustrated by this lack of success; yet if there was any consolation to be taken, it was in the fact that his men were slow, yet knew the terrain well. The intruders would be even slower. They would be more liable to give away their position, where his men would be harder for the enemy to detect.

All of those factors should have helped reassure him that his men would be able to root out the American and his Lagos team and dispose of any threat they offered before they reached base. It was regrettable that military men should also perish, but that was their problem. All but one of them were not allied to the Brotherhood and so would have been under guard by tomorrow in any case. As for the man who was a brother and who had so far not fulfilled his task, that was his own fault, no one else's.

Ehurie had always dealt with everything in his life head-on and hand to hand. He ran his criminal businesses personally, making fear of his own iron will a weapon that he used often. In the same way, the membership of the Brotherhood of the Eagle had seen that hands-on approach, and he had risen swiftly through the ranks as his blend of pragmatism and violence had proved effective. So it pained him—almost physically, if the ache in his gut was anything to go by—that he was forced to sit there, manning the comm link, while others blundered and screwed up in the field.

So when the message came through, it was too much for him to resist. A detail on the eastern sector of the forest reported signs of movement a few hundred meters from where they were searching.

The commander sat forward, barely daring to breathe while he listened for progress. Word came through in that way: literally one word at a time, as his men closed silently on the suspected enemy position.

Ehurie knew where they were. He could not resist being in at the kill. He barked an order for the detail leader to keep him informed and grabbed a handset, tuning it so that he could receive directly from the communications center. He descended rapidly from the treetop building, rushing to the ordnance hut to equip himself with more than the small arms he carried as a matter of course. As he went, he issued an order to the duty guard to cover the command of base until he returned.

He grabbed an AK-47, a MAC-10, some ammunition and a web belt loaded with fragmentation and explosive grenades. He fumbled as he fitted it, the adrenaline pumping through him. Was it a sense of purpose or just revenge? Maybe both. He only knew that he had to be in on the kill.

That explained the sense of exhilaration that flowed through him when he heard that the detail was firing on the enemy party and had the men pinned down. It explained the order that would later seem to be so self-destructive.

"I want all details to that point. We take them down. Take them down hard," he snarled into his radio as he plunged into the forest, forgetting that he needed to retain the detachment of a commanding officer, knowing only that he scented blood.

17

Dirt and grass kicked up around Bolan's head, small stones flying through the air around him along with chippings from larger rocks that whined as they were caught by the random fire. He was still alive, still unharmed. He hadn't heard any cries that made him think that others of his team were dead.

It was spray'n'pray time. The Brotherhood fighters knew roughly where his men were located, and although they had pinned them down, they had no real notion of where they were within this area.

So there was hope. All he needed was something to break the cycle that they were trapped in. Bolan had to take a chance.

Still keeping his head down, and painfully aware that their limited choice of firepower kept his options narrowed, the big American removed a grenade from his web belt. He pulled the pin and scrambled to his knees just long enough to arm the bomb and toss it toward the area where the gunfire originated before dropping back down to cover.

He counted silently and equalized his jaw for any pressure in the relatively enclosed outdoor space as the grenade went off. The floor of the forest shook under the impact while earth, grass, rock and wood poured over them. Any screams of pain or death were lost in the all-encompassing roar of the blast, but the sudden cessation of gunfire in the aftermath told its own story.

With caution, Bolan raised his head and scrambled into a crouch. Hunkered down, he could see his men, with equal caution, rising from their own positions. Smoke and dust drifted across the space between them as the debris from the blast settled, and through the curtain, Bolan beckoned his men.

As they advanced, weapons raised, alert for any movement, it was the silence around them that was the most awe inspiring. It was as though a cone of silence had descended over this section of the forest, birds and animals gone or in hiding, and men either unconscious or dead.

A few yards from where they had been hiding, in the direction of the blast, they came across the division of men—eight in all—who had pinned them down. Six were dead, of which half of them had been shredded by shrapnel. Two were left alive. Both had been rendered unconscious but were now showing signs of coming round.

Bolan took one of them and shook him roughly to wake him. The man's eyes opened, but they lacked focus.

"How many of you are there?" he growled in a low voice. From the way the man looked, he wasn't seriously expecting a reply. He was right; he didn't get one. He let the enemy fighter drop back to the ground.

"Which way?" he snapped.

Ekwense indicated the signs of a path that the opposition had hacked through the undergrowth. "We'd better get going, Cooper," he said. "There will be more."

"Yeah, but how many?" Bolan wondered out loud. Being outnumbered in unfamiliar terrain, he would have preferred to have known the odds. Still, he trusted his men.

What happened behind him made him question that. He heard a gurgling sound and turned to see that Saro Wiwa had cut the throat of the man he had questioned and was in the act of disposing of the other live soldier. The heavy-set military man stopped midstroke on seeing Bolan stare.

"Leave no one. We cannot risk them tracking us."

Bolan was never comfortable with such reasoning, but it was too late to question now; that could come later. He nodded and indicated that they move, not trusting himself to say anything.

Bolan's party moved into the dark recesses of the forest without looking back, leaving the carnage behind them, in search of their target.

WHEN EHURIE CAUGHT up with his men, he knew what he would find. He had followed the sound of gunfire and then taken cover when the explosion sounded. In the sudden silence that followed, he had a sinking feeling in his gut. One that was only confirmed when he reached the site of the blast, where the other detail he had dispatched had also just arrived.

"How can the American outsmart us so easily?" he berated them, his anger sparking in all directions. "This is our land. We know this forest. We must defeat him and his traitors."

"Sir, they must go that way," one of his men said, almost too scared to speak in the face of Ehurie's anger.

"Why?" the commander barked.

"There is no other trail," he answered in a tremulous voice.

Ehurie grunted and nodded. "Then we go. Find them. Kill them."

He pushed ahead of his detail and took point as he plunged into the undergrowth with little pretense at delicacy. The American's men would know he was in pursuit. Let them sweat. He would go through them no matter what they threw at him.

KEN WAS AT the rear of the party, and was the first to hear their pursuers crashing through the undergrowth. He whispered to Emecheta, just ahead of him, to wait and listen. The military man passed the message down the line until it reached Bolan. Like all his men, he paused to hear the approaching soldiers and gauged their distance.

"Take cover. We'll ambush them. Victor, move on and make it look like we're still ahead."

"Man, I never thought I looked like a goat to you," Ekwense muttered with a grin that was as much fueled by fear as humor, but he knew his task. He forged ahead at a quicker pace, wanting to get some space between himself and the enemy on his tail. At the same time he made sure that he beat down the path to make it look as though more than one man was walking ahead, making more noise than he would on his own to deceive those just out of sight.

While he did that, the remaining men melted into the forest around the trail. It was densely packed in this part and provided enough cover as long as a person was able to negotiate the maze of branches, vines and roots that made for such a wall. Bolan picked his way through it, like all of them unwilling to make a path that was easily discernible. It did little to make their task simple, and it was a race against time to find effective cover.

It was close and uncomfortable in the thick undergrowth that enveloped them. Bolan could not see any of his men, which was good, but by the same token left him uncertain to positioning in the event of a firefight. He would have to hope for the best, should it come to that. Sweat soaked his back and neck, and he wiped it from his forehead with a sleeve that was already damp in the humidity. Insects buzzed perpetually around him, and as he could not swat them, he could only hope that any bites were not toxic.

The enemy approached at double time. They were making no attempt to recon, and that recklessness only puzzled the soldier. His puzzlement dissolved as the enemy came into view. Bolan recognized the thunder-faced Ehurie from a description Ekwense had given him.

The solider had the gangster Brotherhood commander buttoned as a hothead, used to things going his way and inclined to fly into a rage if that was not the case. It looked like Bolan was proved right. He knew Ehurie was at least part of the high command, if not commander of the base, and for him to act like this was suicidal and stupid.

So be it.

As the detail Ehurie led hit the center of the path where Bolan's men were located, they were suddenly hit by a volley of shots that took out three men immediately. Unable to risk rapid fire because of their own men located in the undergrowth opposite, the fighters had taken single-shot aim to thin the ranks and, before the enemy had a chance to react, had burst from their hiding places to engage in hand-to-hand combat.

Bolan had fired one shot and seen it pluck at Ehurie's sleeve, throwing the shaved-headed commander off balance, and make it impossible for Bolan to accurately sight and risk a second shot. Cursing, the big American made to break cover and take on the enemy leader.

It was only at that moment that he realized that his attention had been too narrowly focused. He felt the sour breath on his cheek and the iron grip of the arm that encircled his chest before the blade of the knife settled at his throat. The soldier who had him in his grasp was pushed up against him, enabling Bolan to guess who he was from his height and body mass.

"You. The only one?" he asked in a whisper that was far calmer than the adrenaline pumping through his system should have allowed.

"Only me. Only need for one."

"You took your time." Bolan wanted to keep him talking, each second allowing his mind to race, his muscles to instinctively flex and look for a weak spot in the grip.

"Just need to be rid of you."

"What about the base?" Bolan asked.

"What about it? Just a communications point. It can be sacrificed to the greater good."

"Those were your orders?"

"If necessary. Not that it matters to you."

Bolan felt his grip tighten, the knife start to dig as the blade rotated ready to slice across his neck. It meant that the man behind him had raised his arm slightly, allowing just enough room for Bolan to act. It opened up the body of his attacker so that Bolan could flex the elbow that was not totally enclosed in a grip, driving it up so that it rammed into his opponent's ribs and the hollow between the rib cage and the shoulder joint. At the same time he raked the heel of his combat boot down the man's shin, weakening his stance on the opposite side.

The knife raked up and across Bolan's face, catching the top of his ear as he bobbed and weaved. He felt the air move as it crossed in front of his eye, the merest fraction from blinding him. It was enough of a margin. He pushed away and made some space, turning awkwardly while still in the man's grip to come face-to-face with Saro Wiwa. The density of the woodland pushed them close together so that Bolan was looking directly into the cold, dead eyes of the Brotherhood traitor.

There was no time, nor was there room, for him to draw a weapon. He would have to rely on his skills alone. He feinted and weaved as the military man thrust at him, adept enough to avoid any attempt at blocking or disabling his knife hand.

As Saro Wiwa thrust at him, instead of feinting Bolan stepped into the blow, trusting his timing to duck beneath it. He slammed his hard-edged hand into the military man's groin, following it with a hammer blow to the side of his head as Saro doubled with the sudden agony. The big American sank on top of him as he fell, delivering repeated blows to the head, pinning his knife arm beneath a knee. Saro Wiwa struggled, but was disoriented and wild in striking out. Bolan snatched the knife from his hand and with the same momentum thrust it into the military man's neck. The cold, dead eyes were now just that.

Breathing heavily, Bolan was aware that a pitched battle was still going on at his rear. Rising and gulping down air, he pushed through the undergrowth and into the fray.

In the chaos, it was easy to note that his men had the upper hand. The only casualty was Kanu, who was on the ground. The man he had been fighting lay beside him. Bolan's men had used their pangas and knives, and their superior numbers had allowed them to take out the Brotherhood men with some ease. Bolan left his men to their mopping up and moved over to where Kanu lay. The ground around him was soaked with blood from a gut wound that was deep and incisive. Bolan tried to make him comfortable.

The lanky fighter's eyes were glassy and faraway, finding it hard to focus on Bolan as he leaned over him. The Nigerian's voice was likewise distant, words coming faintly and as though through fog.

"Don't worry, Cooper. I'm done. So's that bastard. Look after my boys, let them get home."

There was nothing Bolan could say to him. He nodded, promised to look after Kanu's family and watched the light fade from the man's eyes.

An exchange of gunfire up ahead distracted him. Ekwense. The cab-driving fighter had not tracked back but had taken cover to stop any of the enemy who escaped the ambush. A look around showed Bolan that Ehurie—the man he should have taken out if Saro Wiwa had not distracted him—was not among the casualties.

Bolan cursed and set off at a run toward the sound of gunfire, racking his SMG in readiness. He could feel, rather than see, the cab driver's fellow fighters at his heels.

The overgrown path twisted and turned, and they could not see what had happened until they were virtually on top of where Ekwense lay. He was twisted, with his SMG laying just out of reach, stitched from shoulder to groin by gunfire. His eyes were staring wide, and his lips curled back over his teeth in the rictus smile of death.

"That bastard will pay for this," Samuel breathed, stopping abruptly behind Bolan as the soldier leaned over their dead comrade.

"He may already have," Bolan commented, indicating the trail of blood that led away along the path. "Victor wasn't the only one hit."

"Let him stay alive long enough," Samuel snarled. He leaned over Ekwense, closing his eyes. "Goodbye, old friend. I will look after Charity for you." He looked up, along the path. "Let's get the son of a bitch."

Bolan laid a hand on his arm. "Not at our own expense. Stay calm, Samuel, especially if you want to look after his family. Okay?"

The fighter looked at Bolan, for a moment his eyes far away, before he snapped back to the present. He nodded with a grunt before getting to his feet. He looked around. "Who else have we lost besides Victor and Kanu?"

"Saro Wiwa," Bolan said quickly. "Stray shot got the poor bastard. Didn't have a chance." He did not want to explain what had really happened and risk dissent or disillusion among the remaining men. "We do this for the three of them, okay?"

The assembled men agreed, and Bolan led them off at double time, headed toward the base camp and the final encounter. So far they had seen off around twenty men. How many were left for them to fight?

EHURIE LIMPED, STUMBLED and ran the rest of the way back to camp. He had nailed that bastard who had stepped out on him, but not before he had taken shots in the left shoulder and arm, which now hung helpless at his side as he approached the first guard post.

Two men rushed out to greet him, supporting and half carrying him the rest of the way back. The guard he had left in charge saw them approach and came running with a medical kit. Dragged into the shelter of a hut, Ehurie was laid out by his men, and had to gasp for breath and to speak as his wounds were dressed as well as possible.

"They're on their way," he croaked. "Pull all remaining men back to this circle. Go call Abiola. Tell him to put contingency plans into operation as communications may go down. Tell him his planted man was shit. The American is still alive. He can get back to Lagos in time, if we don't stop him, but they must be ready."

He fell back, the effort and the pain exhausting him. He was aware that the guard he had made officer-in-charge had rushed out to fulfill his orders. The other two guards hovered over him. A burst of anger fueled him enough to rise on his good arm.

"What the hell are you doing here? Get out—you have a base to defend…" He sank back with the effort, almost sobbing as he sucked in breath. The two guards saluted him and hurried out.

Ehurie had a sinking feeling that the revolution was

going to go ahead without him. After all that work, he would miss out. It was one of the few things that could make him cry. He could feel the tears of self-pity and frustration well up.

They did not come.

The brace of explosions, so close together that they were almost as one echo of another, jolted him out of his slough of despondency.

The American was here....

18

As they approached the base, the track opening out, Bolan
and his men were brought up short by volleys of fire that
raked the dirt before them. They were fortunate that the
men before them were nervous and jumpy, firing just a
fraction before their enemy came into range and so giving them the early warning necessary to duck back and
take cover.

The forest on either side of the hacked-out path was still
dense, but a little thinner than where they had mounted
the ambush, making it easier for them to take some kind
of cover. While four of the men set up a covering fire,
Bolan indicated that he would undertake a recon. He did
more than that. As he moved forward through the undergrowth, he could see that the base—a cleared area that lay
only a few yards from his position—was in chaos, with
men running around trying to mount a guard, secure huts
that presumably housed ordnance and equipment of some
kind and find cover as they were spooked by the sudden
flurry of fire.

It was evident to Bolan that the ranks of Brotherhood
fighters at this base had been thinned considerably. Rather
than return to his men and waste time briefing them, he
opted to act and trust that they would have the sense to follow. He took two grenades and launched them from where

he stood, having adjusted his position to give him the necessary space for throwing. He didn't worry if that attracted attention. It would only add to the imminent confusion.

The grenades went off almost simultaneously, followed by the dull *whump* of fuel igniting as one of the trucks was caught by the blast, fire spreading across the dry tarp on its flatbed and reaching drums of fuel stored beneath.

Some of the enemy had been taken out by the double blast, but those who had remained on their feet had more resilience—fear-fueled adrenaline, perhaps—than he had hoped. He had to move through the bush quickly to avoid the fire that raked the foliage around him, diving low and rolling painfully over roots and branches to get beyond the trail of raking slugs.

He came up onto his feet, second nature guiding the SMG to his hands, set to burst mode. He moved forward to engage, knowing from the sound of fire that came from back of him that his men had taken their cue without needing to be told.

In the center of the base camp, the few men who remained from the Brotherhood details had regrouped and were taking cover where they could, returning fire and consolidating rather than taking the fight forward. Two of them were frantically trying to extinguish the fire around the truck, intent on preventing it from spreading to one of the huts. Bolan realized that that had to house ordnance, fuel or something else of an explosive potential. Let them deal with the fire; they could wait.

Moving from cover to cover, Bolan edged forward, exchanging fire, taking one yard, two yards at a time, forcing the enemy back farther until they were clustered around the base of the trees that housed the treetop huts. It didn't take much to realize that this was where the communications were based.

Risking attracting gunfire to make a head count of his men as far as he could see, he noted that Emecheta and Obinna were missing, as was Samuel. He could see one man—military by the fatigues he wore—lying half-concealed in the bush. He could not tell which of the men it was.

The enemy, on the other hand, was being thinned out rapidly. Their orders had made it necessary for them to retreat into a position that left them with little option except to keep firing and praying that they would run out of opposition before they ran out of allies.

As Bolan watched, astonished, Ehurie reeled from one of the buildings. He was swathed in bandages, stumbled and staggered across the open ground between the hut and the area where his men were clustered. He carried an Uzi, which he balanced awkwardly in one hand, the other hanging limp at his side. He fired random bursts of fire that knocked him farther off balance than he was already, the fire going wide and spraying around the edge of the compound clearing.

He lasted a few seconds, probably because the sight of him was so arresting that it took that long for his enemies to take in what they were seeing. Once they had snapped out of it, a hail of fire was paid to the deranged commander. Bolan figured that the members of his Lagos team were the primary shooters, extracting revenge on the man who had killed their friends.

The fight might have gone out of his men as he fell, but in a perverse sense, Ehurie's death just spurred them on. He may be gone, but they could not let down the Brotherhood in which they believed. The hail of fire increased in intensity, and Bolan wondered how long it would take to crack them. Time was not something he had on his side.

His question was answered sooner than he expected.

Obinna and Samuel appeared from behind the trees at the far side of the compound. Any guards that had stayed back there had evidently been no match for their determination, and they were unexpected by the men who were concentrating on the enemy before them. Making little effort at concealment, concentrating on rapid fire and movement, the two men moved across the space, cutting down the Brotherhood fighters before they had a chance to react and return fire.

When it was over, there was a moment of silence before Bolan's men realized that they were the only ones left standing; they had won.

But there was no time for celebration. Work remained to be done. The two men who had been attending the fire had now put it out, and were standing with their hands aloft. Without weapons, they had decided that discretion was truly the better, if not only, part of valor. Sosimi and Ken grabbed them, pulling them over to Bolan.

The fight had gone from them. They answered his questions without hesitation, and before long, he was up in the tree hut that housed the communications center. Samuel stood beside him as he looked over the equipment.

"I expected more fight, more men," Samuel murmured.

"This is a front," Bolan said as he carefully disconnected the network, leaving the Brotherhood a web with no spider in the center. "All communication is filtered through here, but the idea that this is the headquarters of the organization is a crock of shit."

"Like a card trick. Find the lady and watch the wrong hand... Then where is the leader? You know." The last was not a question.

Bolan looked Samuel in the eye. "You know I checked my smartphone before we entered the forest? I was given intel that the leak that nearly stopped the mission had been traced. When I saw who was responsible, then I understood. But we had to take this base down before I could cut the head off the Brotherhood. I didn't lead you wrong."

"Then where do we go from here?"

"We need to get back to Lagos."

"We have the chopper," Samuel interrupted. "Lagos? All this time? We will take you."

"When we get there, it might—"

"When we get there, then I will come with you, Cooper. Do not argue with me." There was something about Samuel's tone, and the look in his eye, that convinced Bolan it would be pointless to try.

He thought he knew why, and the lanky fighter's next words confirmed it. "Victor and me were children in the area. I knew him since we were both young boys. I will grow old without him. Someone will pay for that."

Bolan nodded slowly. "I understand. But you have to understand that this is about the country, not just Victor. Let me lead the way, and we'll see justice served."

Samuel was impassive. "It had better be."

The two men, having disabled and destroyed key components in the system, went back to ground level, where they found that their men were clustered in the center of the compound, making use of provisions they had found, the two prisoners shackled in the middle of the group.

"No time for this," Samuel called as they descended. "We have to go—Cooper will explain on the way," he added, seeing the expressions on Ken and Achuaba's faces.

"You men," Bolan said, addressing the military team. "I want you to go back to the air strip. Captain Shonekan is an odd man, but he's loyal to the government. He suspects some of his own men. We can't let word escape, so help him secure them and wait for word before you leave."

"What about you?" Ayinde asked.

"You don't need me," Bolan said, clapping him on the shoulder. "None of those Brotherhood bastards will get past you. I've got to get back to Lagos quickly and quietly. I've work to do, and these men are best to follow me as they have no official status. You'll have to trust my judgment."

Ayinde shrugged. "It's been fair up till now."

One of the trucks in the camp was still working. Bolan took it, with Samuel, Ken and Achuaba, leaving the military men and their prisoners to trek back to the savanna, where they still had a truck to carry them back to the air strip. It would take time, but that would suit Bolan's purpose.

The journey back to the Huey, the refueling and the first leg of the flight back were carried out in virtual silence. The empty seats where Ekwense and Kanu should have been sitting loomed over the remaining men. Bolan assisted in the flight, but felt a ghostly presence on his shoulder.

It was only when they made the second refueling stop, precarious in the dark, that they began to discuss what had happened and what Bolan proposed to do on their return to Lagos. It took some persuasion for Ken and Achuaba to agree to return to their families and the families of those who would not return. They trusted Bolan—more importantly they knew that Samuel would ensure that justice, however rough, was meted out.

The early morning sun was rising as they reached the small airfield where they had departed only a day before, a day that seemed like a lifetime. Leaving Ken and Achuaba to attend to the old man at the hangars, Samuel and Bolan took the car that had been left behind and drove into a Lagos that was just awakening to a day that would not unfold as some had planned....

Milton Abiola had been at his desk since the previous evening. Only snatched moments of sleep, some pills and coffee to keep him going, and the end was in sight. In a few short hours the coup would be in operation, and Oruma would assume his rightful position as the head of Nigeria. The old man had been treated shamefully and dismissed by the military regime that he had done so much to put in place, and his reputation as a maverick and loose cannon had led to the post-military regime distancing themselves from him, despite the hero status he held from the days of Biafra. Once he assumed command, Abiola was convinced that the people would rejoice. The only thing concerning him was the fall of the communications system. That did not matter. Oruma's broadcast to the nation once the transmitters had been seized would be enough. Still, if that fool Ehurie had failed, and the man Oboko had infiltrated proved as useless as the man who had sent him, then it meant that the American was still alive.

But too far away to be a problem. He could be dealt with in due course.

Abiola drew the blinds in his office and blinked at the rising sun. He would go and check on the old man, who always arrived early at the ministry, but was more likely to today of all days.

Abiola left his office and pushed the button for the elevator. He was wrapped up in thought and did not notice the two men approach him from the rear as the doors opened. He did not register what had happened to him until his face was pressed up against the cold metal wall of the elevator.

"Major, you will take us to your leader, if you don't mind," Bolan whispered in his ear.

"How the hell—"

"Did we get here? Ingenuity and determination. By the

way, if you were going to be around for any longer, I'd tell you how useless your night security is. But your time's up."

The elevator door opened, and Samuel led them out, Bolan keeping Abiola in an armlock. The corridor was empty. Outside Oruma's office, Bolan knocked once. Abiola opened his mouth, but found it hard to talk through the barrel of Samuel's AK-47. A muffled voice from within bade them to enter.

As they strode in, Oruma's secretary, openmouthed in shock, rose from her desk. For such a prim-and-proper middle-aged woman she was quick with a Mauser, which she pulled clear of her desk drawer as she rose. She had it leveled at Bolan and Abiola but had no chance to act on her intent as Samuel took her out with one shot from the AK-47. It sounded deafening in the quiet room and drowned any sound she made as she hit the wall.

Bolan indicated to Samuel to open the inner door and stand to one side. As Samuel did so, Bolan thrust Abiola forward. The major stumbled forward, unable to stop himself as the armlock was released. He tried to speak, as he knew what was about to happen, was too slow and powerless to stop it. As he barreled through the doorway, three shots from a Glock stitched his chest.

Bolan and Samuel used this diversion to swiftly enter the office, each man moving either side of the doorway to split the target.

Oruma stood behind his desk, the Glock pointed down. With cold fury and hate, he looked from Samuel to Bolan and back.

"Try it," Bolan said calmly. "You shoot one of us, the other takes you down. You really want to die?"

Oruma smiled as he slowly put his gun on his desk. "You cannot stop me. Even if you imprison me, my followers will now know me, and they will free me or wait for me. Better a live martyr than a dead one."

"I wouldn't bet on that," Bolan said coldly. "Once the sham of the Brotherhood is exposed as just a sordid vehicle for your fantasies of gaining power, the thing that binds all the fanatics together will go. It's idealism, not people, that they want."

"We shall see," Oruma mused. "You know, it is a pity that you are such a self-righteous prig. Maybe you and I could have made an alliance."

"Flattery will get you nowhere," Bolan replied. "Now just come out from behind the desk and lie on the floor."

Oruma looked at him, confused.

"Hey, indulge a self-righteous prig," the solider said, gesturing with his gun.

With a puzzled expression, Oruma came out from behind the desk and with a difficulty that showed his age, got down onto the floor, arms spread-eagled, face in the carpet.

"Samuel, I've just got to check the corridor. I think you wanted to have a word with our friend here."

Bolan left the room. Samuel stood over the old man.

"The name Victor Ekwense would mean nothing to you," he said in a harsh whisper.

"Is that you, my friend? I can use a man like you, Victor—"

"Be quiet," Samuel snapped, silencing him. "I am not Victor. He was my friend. We ran together, fought together. He is dead because of you. You are a Christian man, you say?"

"Yes," Oruma said hurriedly. "I am sorry to hear of your loss—"

"Do you know the Old Testament, then, as well?" Samuel interrupted. He saw the aged man stiffen. "I see that you know what I mean. Think of this now…."

Samuel leveled the AK-47 and squeezed once. Oruma's body shook in spasm and then was still.

Bolan was waiting in the corridor when Samuel came out.

"There's some mopping up to be done," he said in a matter-of-fact tone. "You up to giving me a hand?"

Samuel nodded. "I am now."

In New York City, Benjamin Williams raised his hands helplessly as he sat opposite Hal Brognola. Adam Mars-Jones sat next to the old man, shaking his head. Two days had passed, and the coup had been strangled at birth, an obscure army captain named Ernest Shonekan being hailed as a national hero for raising an alarm before action had begun.

"I would have trusted Wilson with my life," Williams said sadly. "The man who saved me once before would not have done this. I do not know why—"

"You've been away a long time. Things change," Brognola interrupted gently. "Your integrity is not in doubt."

"But your man—he might have—"

"My man has an unerring nose for the good guys." Brognola grinned. "He found some. When you've got his experience and a few good men, it's surprising what you can do."

* * * * *

Don Pendleton's Mack Bolan.

TERROR BALLOT

The streets of Paris explode when terror becomes a political weapon...

When France's presidential elections are hijacked by terrorists, violence erupts on the streets of Paris, fueling extreme antiforeigner sentiment. The chaos feeds votes to the ultraradical candidate, but intelligence indicates the attacks may be the ultimate propaganda tool. Mack Bolan answers the call of duty, launching a surgical strike against the powerful, skilled radicals carrying out the slaughter. As the city of light bursts into a blaze of cleansing fire, the Executioner casts his vote for the terrorists' blood—and an end to their deadly campaign.

Available March wherever books and ebooks are sold.

Or order your copy now by sending your name, address, zip or postal code, along with a check or money order (please do not send cash) for $6.99 for each book ordered ($7.99 in Canada), plus 75¢ postage and handling ($1.00 in Canada), payable to Gold Eagle Books, to:

In the U.S.
Gold Eagle Books
3010 Walden Avenue
P.O. Box 9077
Buffalo, NY 14269-9077

In Canada
Gold Eagle Books
P.O. Box 636
Fort Erie, Ontario
L2A 5X3

Please specify book title with your order.
Canadian residents add applicable federal and provincial taxes.

GOLD EAGLE ®

GSB164

The Executioner
Don Pendleton's
HANGING JUDGE

Hell hath no fury like a future scorned...

Justice is a damning word in what used to be called
Oklahoma, thanks to a sadistic baron known as the
Hanging Judge. Crazy, powerful and backed by a
despotic sec crew, the judge drops innocents from
the gallows at will. When Jak narrowly escapes, a
rift among the companions sends them deep into the
wilderness outside the ville. Separated and hurting,
time is running out for the survivors to realize they're
stronger together than they ever could be alone—before
a ruthless madman brings them to the end of their rope.

Available in March, wherever books and ebooks are sold.

**GOLD
EAGLE** ®